THE CAD, THE COUCH, AND THE CUT DIRECT

JESSIE LEWIS

Quills & Quartos
PUBLISHING

Edited by Kristi Rawley and Jo Abbott

Cover design by Hoja Designs

ISBN 978-1-963213-03-4 (ebook) 978-1-963213-04-1 (paperback)

To anyone who ever wanted to spend just a little more time
with Darcy and Elizabeth

CONTENTS

PROLOGUE

On a warm and otherwise innocuous Friday evening in June, Mr Fitzwilliam Darcy entered the British Institution in Pall Mall, London. Therein was displayed a collection of works by several celebrated artists, and splendid were the many exhibits. That, however, was not why Darcy had come. Up the grand staircase and through a series of candlelit rooms he moved, navigating his way with ill-disguised impatience around groups of milling connoisseurs, dilettantes, and proponents of fashionable society. He searched the faces around him, anxious to catch a glimpse of his quarry but increasingly certain he had missed his chance—until he reached the entrance of the upper east exhibition room.

There, beyond a sea of tables, easels, floor candelabras, and what seemed like half the *ton*, seated on one very particular couch, between two architecturally extraneous but nevertheless imposing marble columns, sat Miss Elizabeth Bennet.

He breathed a sigh of relief to see her there, and to see that she was alone. She looked extraordinarily lovely, the glow of so many candles adding yet another layer of loveliness to her complexion. He knew he must speak to her, yet his feet remained obstinately rooted to the spot. This might be the last time he ever saw her, the last moment before the spark of hope that flickered wildly in his breast was forever doused. He would look his fill before he chanced to hear her say that all hope was in vain.

It had been more than half a year since he last spoke to her—at an excruciating dinner at Longbourn the previous autumn—and they had scarcely exchanged a dozen words on that occasion. He had gone there to judge whether he might ever succeed in making Elizabeth love him.

To his profound regret, it had transpired that no, he could not.

In the eight months since, his admiration and regard for her had not lessened by even the smallest iota, and misery and loneliness had become his constant bedfellows. What Elizabeth had done in those eight months, and with whom she had done it, Darcy knew not. What he did know was that now she was in danger, and he could not—nay, *would* not—stand by and allow her to be ill-used.

She might not thank him for it, he knew. The cost of his previous interference had been the loss of her regard—or at least the entrenching of her antipathy. Yet the cost of his silence where Wickham was concerned had been greater still, and to more people than him alone. Thus, although he did not relish drawing Elizabeth's ire upon himself again, he would warn her that she was about to ally herself with a different cad.

He would have done so, even if her displeasure were guaranteed. There was, however, one tiny sliver of hope that she might not be displeased to see him. As a consequence of the most unlikely sequence of events ever to have occurred in—or out of, for that matter—an art gallery, an astonishing report had reached him: that against all evidence to the contrary, Elizabeth might be amenable to a renewal of his attentions.

So incredible was this string of coincidences that Darcy could scarcely believe it had happened at all, let alone what it purportedly signified. And yet, had none of it come to pass in the manner it had, he would never have learnt to hope at all. He would have turned away from this exact spot—where, four days ago, he had set eyes on Elizabeth for the first time in months—and left without ever seeing her again. Fortunately, that was not quite how events transpired.

CHAPTER ONE

Earlier that week

D arcy had never stared at a painting with such intensity in his life as the one in front of him, depicting three rotten apples and a dead fish. Other visitors had come and gone, and he had murmured assent to every expression of admiration they had made about it, hoping none of them would notice how often his gaze was not on the canvas at all but beyond it. For, with a furtiveness that was both uncharacteristic and unpardonable, he was watching Elizabeth stroll about the room, arm in arm with a woman he did not know, whilst he attempted to summon the courage to talk to her.

He had not expected to see her here. He had not expected to see her *anywhere*, ever again, and the shock of doing so had apparently knocked all rational thought out of his head. Nothing and no one else could reduce him to cowering out of sight behind an easel in a public viewing gallery, but he knew not how he ought to go about greeting her.

His initial thought had been that he ought not to attempt it at all; she could have no desire to see him, and he certainly had no wish to be mortified by her indifference. As was her wont, however, she had exerted an insuperable gravitational pull on him, and he had found himself approaching—only to divert at the last moment to contemplate the lifeless carp, a less perilous encounter by far.

He willed her to look his way; then he willed her with equal force *not* to, for the possibility that she might see him but choose not to acknowledge him was too painful to countenance. He instantly dismissed the notion; Elizabeth might not return his regard, but that did not alter the fact that she was the most compassionate and amiable woman of his acquaintance. Publicly slighting people was not something she would ever do. That assurance, in addition to the overwhelming desire to speak to her, drew Darcy out from behind the easel.

She and her companion had stopped to peer up at a large seascape hung high on the wall. In profile, with her chin tilted up and a pensive frown on her face, Elizabeth looked so lovely that Darcy smiled despite his unease. He had not forgotten a single feature of her countenance, but memories were no substitute for the real thing, and the real Elizabeth was sublime. His feet moved towards her, his heart began to pound as though he were approaching a lion's den, and then the woman on Elizabeth's arm struck up a conversation with another couple. It was enough to scatter Darcy's tenuous resolve, and he turned away, bumped into someone, apologised, sidestepped them, knocked into someone else, apologised again, and hastened to the opposite wall, cringing lest Elizabeth had heard the commotion and seen him scurrying away.

Damn this insanity! He would leave. He would return to his sister, waiting in the carriage outside, and forget he had ever seen Elizabeth. Except, he was now as far from the main double doors as it was possible to be, on the wrong side of the room to reach the only other exit—a small, single door in the far corner—and so depleted of courage that he could not bring himself to turn around. The painting he had come to be staring at this time was a particularly well-rendered pastiche of *Judith and Holofernes*, only in this one, rather than the woman slitting the man's throat, she was stabbing him in the heart. *Apropos,* he thought wryly.

In truth, though, Elizabeth had not intentionally inflicted any wound on him—his heartbreak was all his own doing. From his careless censure of her beauty, early in their acquaintance, to his profoundly offensive offer of marriage—somewhere in the middle, he had done about as much as any man could to ensure a woman's antipathy. It was little surprise that even his sincerest efforts to redeem himself in the succeeding months had failed.

Had it been up to him, he might never have stopped

believing he would one day succeed in making her love him. He had, after all, fooled himself before into thinking that she did, and the force of the passion he felt for her could easily have led to him being fooled again. Regrettably, there had been a stream of evidence in proof of the fact that all hope was lost, which even his desperate heart had not been able to overlook.

The first blow had come during the few days the previous autumn when he had returned to London to attend to some insignificant business that he wished now he had ignored. He had left Hertfordshire with the expectation that Bingley would propose to Miss Jane Bennet while he was gone and with every intention of returning to try and secure the same happiness for himself with Elizabeth. Before his business was concluded, Lady Catherine had arrived at his London house with the news that she had visited Longbourn and been told that Elizabeth was absolutely, irrevocably decided against him.

Notwithstanding the insolence of his aunt's interference, her report was so accurate, the words and phrasing so like Elizabeth's own, Darcy had found it difficult to discredit. He could perfectly envisage Elizabeth unabashedly asserting that Lady Catherine was not entitled to know her business. He could almost hear her exclaiming at the implication that she and he were not equals. He knew precisely what expression she would have worn as she declared that she was resolved to act in that manner that would constitute her happiness without reference to anyone unconnected to her. He could not easily, therefore, dismiss Lady Catherine's claim that Elizabeth had also frankly and openly given the promise that she would never enter into an engagement with him.

This alone might not have been enough to rob him of all hope, but the very next day, Bingley had slunk back to London with his tail between his legs, despondent and still single. Jane Bennet, it transpired, *had* got engaged, only not to him. In the months of his absence, she had met and fallen in love with a Mr Malcolm. The happiness that Darcy had thought he perceived in her upon Bingley's return had been real, but his friend had not been its object.

"The whole family has forsaken me," Bingley had lamented at the time. "Miss Catherine told me Jane is happier with Malcolm than she ever was with me, and according to her, Miss Elizabeth is delighted that the man has no friends in high places to persuade him against her family."

Until that moment, Darcy had dared to dream that Elizabeth had forgiven him for separating Bingley and Jane. When they met in Derbyshire the previous summer, she had no longer seemed angry. Of course, that was before Wickham eloped with Lydia Bennet. When that news reached them, Elizabeth had hastened home to support her family, and he had raced to London with the purpose of saving her sister. Alas, Miss Lydia had not wanted to be saved, and the best Darcy had managed was to force Wickham to make an honest woman of her. With which act, he had hammered the final nail in the coffin of his own romantic aspirations.

He tried to have as little to do with the Wickhams as possible, but since they moved to Newcastle, he had been required to settle several more debts of honour as well as to vouch—in person—for Wickham's character, to prevent him losing his commission and returning to Longbourn to live off Mr Bennet's meagre income. Whilst Darcy was in Newcastle, Mrs Wickham, far further into her first pregnancy than her few months of marriage made feasible, had railed at him for her pitiful circumstances.

"This is all your fault! You made me marry him! You, who knew he could never be a good husband, made me take him into my bed!"

When Darcy pointed out that she had obviously taken him there long before anyone insisted that they marry, she had replied, "Only because I thought he could be trusted! If you had told us what he really was, I would never have thrown myself into his power! You know it is true. Wickham knows it, my aunt and uncle Gardiner know it. Lizzy knows it."

"Your sister knows of my involvement in this?" he had demanded.

"Of course she does! You think yourself so cunning—well, Lizzy is twice as clever as you. She knows precisely who condemned me to this hell, and it is hell, Mr Darcy. I have not one reason to be happy. I shall never forgive you for it. None of us will."

That was how Darcy discovered that Elizabeth knew he

had ruined her sister's life, and what had finally put paid to any pretensions to winning her heart.

He let his shoulders slump. Whom was he deceiving? Elizabeth would not wish to speak to him, and it would be an egregious imposition to compel her to do so by accosting her in public. He absolutely must leave before she saw him. With a deep breath, which he let out very slowly, he turned to go. The very first thing he saw when he lifted his eyes to the room was Elizabeth's aunt, Mrs Gardiner, meandering about between the exhibits, just inside the large double doors.

Bloody hell!

He whipped back around, intending to leave via the smaller door instead. Only, upon turning in *that* direction, he saw, now seated upon the couch directly behind him, Elizabeth and her companion. Elizabeth began to lift her head, and in a blind panic, Darcy stepped behind one of two large, marble pillars flanking the couch, stubbing his toe as he did so. The pillar made a hollow sound and swayed, revealing itself to be made of plaster and possessing a distinctly inferior equilibrium than its marble counterpart would have had. He grabbed it with both hands to steady it, and thus it was that the master of Pemberley, who abhorred disguise of every sort, found himself hugging a fake Grecian column whilst inadvertently eavesdropping on a most alarming conversation.

"He spends more time than is good for him in gambling dens and gin houses and worse," the unknown woman was saying, "but none of us has ever been able to persuade him against it."

Elizabeth's quiet, "My goodness," prevented Darcy from leaving immediately. She sounded distrustful, and it drove a spike of alarm into his chest.

"Quite! Still, better the devil you know, and a titled cad is a vast improvement on your nameless adversary. I shall tell him to meet you here tomorrow and parade you about the place a bit. He will like that, for you are very pretty—and it will do *you* good to be seen with him."

"How so?"

"It will stop people whispering that you are *persona non grata*."

"But none of these people will be here tomorrow. I cannot see how it will help to have a hundred *different* people see me with Lord Rutherford."

"People talk, no matter where they are, Miss Bennet. It is up to us to make sure they talk about the right thing. Do not look so worried; I am not proposing that you pledge your troth to him here and now. You only need to hang off his arm for a bit until the gossip dies down. But if he did take a shine to you, I am sure you could overlook his faults. If only to please your mother."

"I...I am really not sure—"

"Fie! I have made him sound ten times worse than he is! He is a great favourite, really. You must not allow his more tedious habits to put you off."

Who is this woman? Darcy had not recognised her face, and he was certain he did not know her voice, but he knew he did not like her. She was as officious as Lady Catherine and seemed equally assured of herself. He wished he had paid more attention to what she looked like, for he might at least have been able to describe her to someone else, but his attention had been fixed solely on her companion.

He did not hear Elizabeth's reply, but she must have given her consent to the meeting, for the obnoxious woman said, "Excellent. You will not regret it. I shall tell him to meet you here at noon."

In a resigned voice, Elizabeth agreed, after which both ladies stood up and moved away into the crowd. Without hesitation, Darcy dashed in front of the couch and out of the door in the opposite corner. After getting lost in a warren of passages and empty rooms, he eventually exited the Institution onto a side alley, and found his way back to where his carriage and his sister awaited him at the front of the building.

Georgiana peered at him expectantly. "Did you—"

"Drive on!" he called to the coachman.

His sister made no further comment, perhaps discouraged by the furious scowl he was directing out of the window, but he could scarcely spare the thought to care. Elizabeth had just been coerced into agreeing to an exceedingly ill-advised meeting with a man who had been described as a cad, who inhabited places 'worse than gambling dens'—which could only mean brothels—and who would take pleasure in parading her about like a trinket on his arm. A man whose name was sitting just out of reach of recognition in the back of Darcy's mind, taunting him with its potential significance.

It was enough for Darcy to know he must act. He had not protected Elizabeth or her sisters from Wickham, and the result had been disastrous. He would not make the same mistake again. Yet, having moments before concluded that she could not possibly wish to speak to him, he knew not how he was to help her.

CHAPTER TWO

"You have been very quiet since we left the gallery, Lizzy. Is anything the matter?"

Elizabeth looked at her aunt and away again, quickly. Something *was* the matter—the same thing that had made her almost stumble and trip outside the gallery. The same thing that had caused her heart to race. The same thing that had given her a palpable jolt of happiness whilst simultaneously filling her eyes with unshed tears. She had no wish to talk about it, though. She had lost count of the number of times her aunt Gardiner, or her sister Jane, or her friend Charlotte had told her it was time to cease dwelling on missed opportunities and allow her heart to heal. She did not want to hear it again.

They were walking past the newly completed Somerset House, and she pretended to admire its vast frontage to conceal her disquiet as she answered, "No, nothing. I am a little tired, that is all."

"I see," Mrs Gardiner replied. They walked a little farther in silence before she added, slyly, "It had nothing to do with us almost running into Mr Darcy, then?"

Elizabeth gasped, looking around so quickly she almost tripped a second time, making a mockery of her attempt to feign composure. It had been the most fleeting of glimpses —Mr Darcy had been stepping into his carriage in front of the British Institution at precisely the moment she and her aunt exited, and he had seemed in a rush—but she would recognise him anywhere, and it had most assuredly been him. Such a sighting would, even in ordinary circumstances, have exposed wounds that lay unhealed and unforgotten beneath the thin veneer of her equanimity. In the context of the encounter just compassed inside the gallery, it was even more distressing.

Her aunt nodded. "I thought as much."

"Before you say anything, I was not going to mention it, so there is no need to tell me again all the reasons I must not talk about him."

"Nobody has told you not to talk about him. We would only see you happy again—is that so terrible?"

"Mama would see me married. Whether or not I am happy is by the bye."

Mrs Gardiner winced but did not argue. "In your mother's eyes, being settled and being happy are one and the same. And however wrong she may be, I can tell you she thinks it because the opposite is so often true. Unless one is extremely well connected or extremely rich, then being an unmarried woman and being unhappy *are* one and the same. You will have to allow yourself to love somebody else when the time comes."

"And I am sure I shall," Elizabeth replied wearily. It was not as though she was not trying to forget Mr Darcy. All her aunt, sister, and friend's frustration combined could not equal her own at being thus afflicted eight months after seeing him last, but it seemed her heart was a more obstinate creature even than she, for there he resided still, and no amount of sympathising, warnings, or good sense had thus far succeeded in banishing him.

She supposed it was fair comeuppance that she should have come to love him so thoroughly just as his affections ran dry. She had, after all, treated him abominably for most of their early acquaintance, and never worse than at the moment he opened his heart to her to propose. Yet, love him she did, and in a way she had never loved anyone before; with respect, gratitude, admiration, and—most unfamiliar to her—ardour.

She had given much thought as to when her sentiments had begun to change. His saving Lydia from ruin and her whole family from degradation had obviously fixed him in her mind as the most generous man she had ever known, but in truth, she rather thought she had been half in love with him by then in any case. His housekeeper's liberal praise of him, given when Elizabeth visited Pemberley the previous summer with her aunt and uncle, had opened her eyes to aspects of his character—fine, admirable aspects—that she had never before considered. Nevertheless, she doubted it would have worked to improve her opinion if her enmity had not already begun to wane. His letter to her, in which he explained his history with Wickham and his motive in separating Mr Bingley and Jane, had done away with much of that. It was difficult to persist with a grudge against someone who had proved themselves innocent of all the charges laid against them.

In the end, Elizabeth had come to believe that every feeling of warmth she now held for Mr Darcy could be traced to the days and weeks after his proposal, during which time it dawned on her that, without any encouragement from her, without any material advantage in it for him, and against the certain violent objections of his family and all his friends, Mr Darcy had truly loved her. Anyone who could effortlessly relinquish sentiments built on so poignant a foundation was a better woman than she.

"Have you given any more thought to Mr Knowles's request?" her aunt enquired gently.

Elizabeth sighed and shook her head. Mr Knowles had occasional business with her uncle, and after meeting her several times in Mr Gardiner's warehouses, he had expressed a desire for them to 'become better acquainted'.

"He seems perfectly amiable, but..." But he did not make her stomach squeeze just by looking at her; he did not make her blush when he took a cup of coffee from her hands; he did not speak to her as his equal or make her proud simply to claim his friendship. She had not wanted his attentions before today, and seeing Mr Darcy only further convinced her of it.

Indeed, never mind Mr Knowles; seeing Mr Darcy

confirmed that she was not ready to submit herself to *any* other man's attentions. Which was unfortunate, considering that she had just agreed to meet one in the gallery tomorrow, and that *not* meeting him would give great offence to the lady who had suggested the arrangement as a favour to her. The thought of it set her heart off racing again. Why, oh *why* had she agreed to it?

"But?" her aunt pressed.

"But I do not know whether I like him well *enough*," she answered with some agitation. "And I cannot help but think that if I agree to spend more time with him, it is as good as saying I *do* like him, and that will only make him think he has leave to propose, and then I shall have to accept him regardless of my sentiments, because if I refuse any more offers of marriage, Mama will disown me."

Mrs Gardiner chuckled lightly. "It is unfortunate that he did not express an interest in Kitty. She seemed quite taken with him."

"Kitty is taken with everything in trousers."

"Lizzy," her aunt replied with a half-admonishing smile. "Your sister is under just as much pressure from your mother to marry. If she is going about the business more eagerly than you, who are we to cavil?"

"Who indeed?" Elizabeth replied, a little distractedly, for an idea had occurred to her which, even if it could give no relief to her injured heart, might at least stop it from pounding, ten to the dozen, in her breast.

"Enough talk of troublesome men," Mrs Gardiner said after another period of silence. "Let us put them all from our minds. What say you we enjoy a little shopping on our way home?"

Elizabeth agreed that she would like that very well and was reasonably happy with her success at concealing the fact that she thought about little else *but* men and their attendant troubles for the entirety of their excursion.

CHAPTER THREE

Colonel Fitzwilliam had accepted his cousin's summons, assuming he wished to discuss Georgiana. She had recently turned seventeen, and as her joint guardians, Darcy and he had agreed it was time she was out in society. It being her first Season, and they both being men, the enterprise was proving somewhat perplexing for all of them.

But Georgiana, it seemed, was not the issue presently on his cousin's mind. Sitting in a comfortable wingback chair in Darcy's study, Fitzwilliam watched him pace up and down, perturbed to see him thus affected by the mere sight of Miss Elizabeth Bennet. He knew Darcy had been badly burnt—not only by her rejection, but by his subsequent failure to improve her opinion of him—but the matter had nevertheless seemed closed. Many months had passed since Darcy conceded defeat and abandoned all hope of securing her affections, and it had been a long time since he had so much as mentioned her name.

"I must say, your disquiet surprises me," Fitzwilliam said carefully. "I assumed your regard for her would have begun to wane by now."

His cousin did not reply.

"Is this not, in part, why you have come to London? I thought you agreed it was time to put yourself about a bit, meet some other women."

"I am here for Georgiana's coming out. If any notions exist of me being 'put about', they were decided by your mother alone."

"She has a point, though. You will have to start thinking about marrying soon. You are not getting any younger."

"Neither are you."

"*I* do not need an heir."

Darcy came to an abrupt halt and fixed him with a dark glower. "Fitzwilliam, I did not ask you here to talk about my future progeny. I asked you here because I need your help."

Fitzwilliam splayed his hands in a defensive gesture. "A thousand pardons. I am at your service. Tell me what it is you need." He crossed his arms and listened, with increasing amusement, as his eminently sensible, Cambridge-educated, universally respected cousin explained that he had inadvertently wedged himself behind some plaster of Paris theatre scenery to avoid having to talk to a woman.

"You have convinced me," he said when Darcy finished speaking. "Never mind being put about—you ought not to be allowed out in public at all. You are a menace to society."

"How so?"

"You cannot go about eavesdropping on young ladies' conversations. You will get yourself a reputation!"

"I did not deliberately eavesdrop—I was trying to avoid her notice. But you are missing the point. Did you not hear what I said about the man she agreed to meet?"

"No, I was too busy enjoying the image you painted." Fitzwilliam receded somewhat when, rather than getting nettled, his cousin grew observably more distressed. "Forgive me. Tell me again—Miss Bennet was talking to whom, about what?"

Darcy rubbed a hand over his face. "I did not recognise the woman, but the man she was describing made Wickham sound like a saint by comparison—a gambler, a rake, and a sot."

"Why on earth did Miss Bennet agree to meet him in that case?"

"Her companion made a joke of it—said he was not that bad and was actually a great favourite."

"Well then. Perhaps there is nothing to worry about."

He shook his head. "Except I recognised the name, Fitzwilliam, and I think there *is* something to worry about."

"And the name is...?"

"Rutherford. It is maddeningly familiar, but I cannot think where I have heard it."

Regrettably, the name was familiar to Fitzwilliam also. "*Lord* Rutherford?" Darcy nodded, and he winced. "I think I know it, too—and if it is the same Rutherford, then I am afraid I do recall hearing it said that he is something of a cad."

"Damn!" Darcy resumed his pacing. "I was hoping you would tell me I had misheard, and actually, he was a fine gentleman."

"Really?" Fitzwilliam asked sceptically. "Your regard for Miss Bennet is very clearly unabated. I find it hard to believe you would be pleased by the prospect of an upstanding young nobleman, sweeping her off her feet."

"I should infinitely prefer it to hearing that she has agreed to meet a bloody whoremonger!" he retorted fiercely.

Fitzwilliam conceded with a nod of his head. Evidently, far from having overcome his attachment, Darcy remained as unreasonably concerned for, as vehemently defensive of, and as violently in love with Elizabeth Bennet as he had been a twelvemonth ago. He knew from experience there would be no talking his cousin out of it. "Well then, what do you intend to do about it?"

"I do not intend to do anything. I was hoping *you* would agree to warn her."

"Me?"

Darcy stood still again and nodded. The daylight had faded to the point where they really ought to have lit some candles, but neither of them had, and his face was shrouded in shadows. His eyes nevertheless gleamed with urgency.

It was an urgency Fitzwilliam did not share. Miss Bennet was a delightful young woman, but she had made her choice. Her happiness was no longer any business of his. "Why must I be involved? Warn her yourself."

"I cannot. She wants nothing to do with me."

"I hate to state the obvious, old boy, but that rather puts paid to your notions of gallantry. You must leave her to make her own mistakes."

"*Mistakes*? Fitzwilliam, if we were talking about her wearing unsuitable shoes for bad weather or taking a wrong turn through town, I might understand that remark. We are talking about a woman's *safety*."

"Granted, but she is by no means friendless. Let her family look after her. It is not your concern, no matter how dearly you obviously wish it were."

"They do not know the danger. Just as they did not know about Wickham—because I considered it beneath me to warn them."

"Then call on Mr Gardiner and warn *him*."

With a heavy sigh, Darcy dropped into a chair and ran a hand through his hair. "I have told you—Elizabeth wants nothing to do with me. I cannot simply appear at her uncle's house and begin dishing out edicts on whom she ought and ought not to associate with. She would resent the interference."

"Ah. Now I begin to see."

Darcy's ultimately successful machinations to separate his friend Bingley from Jane Bennet had been among the chief grounds for Miss Elizabeth Bennet's antipathy towards him. Yet, both parties had since married other people, and to the best of Fitzwilliam's knowledge, at least one of them was content. He had heard of far worse outcomes in marriage and could not agree that there was much basis for anyone to hold a grudge over it still.

"Surely Miss Bennet has forgotten that old grievance by now."

"If she has, that is even less reason for me to want to remind her of it," Darcy replied. "That is why I was hoping you would agree to speak to her."

"Darcy, sending me to do your bidding still constitutes interfering. It would be more honest to speak to her yourself."

He opened his mouth as though to object then closed it again and averted his gaze. "I cannot face it," he said at length. "How do you think I ended up behind the blasted pillar in the first place? I know she does not want me—I have no desire to see it writ all over her face. But I feel too much to do nothing. Do not make me beg, Fitzwilliam. Will you help me or not?"

"Of course I shall," he said quietly, rueful of having made sport of the matter. "What would you like me to do?"

Darcy sighed with obvious relief, a smile dancing briefly at the corner of his mouth before his countenance was once more overtaken with gravity. "She has arranged to meet this Rutherford fellow at the gallery tomorrow at noon. Will you go—try to intercept? She knows you, and she knows you helped me deal with Wickham. If you could somehow let it be known that Rutherford is not to be trusted, she will listen to you, I am sure of it."

Fitzwilliam gave him a decisive nod. "Consider it done."

"Thank you. It means a great deal to me."

"Good. You can pay me in advance with dinner. Come on." He stood up and marched to the door, all anticipation for a hearty meal and some livelier conversation.

CHAPTER FOUR

"Kitty, before you blow the candles out—" Elizabeth hastened into the bedroom that she had always used to share with Jane but was on this visit sharing with one of her younger sisters. Unlike Kitty, who had excused herself to go to bed some time ago, Elizabeth had struggled to extricate herself politely from the conversation between her aunt and uncle and their dinner guests, and she was glad to catch her sister still awake.

"There is something I would talk to you about."

Kitty nevertheless proceeded to snuff one of the two candles out. "If you mean to continue berating me for spilling the wine—"

"I did not *berate* you, I only asked you to take more care. But no, it has nothing to do with that. Please, listen."

Kitty grudgingly put the snuffer down and shuffled

back to lean against her headboard, her legs bent up and her arms crossed over her knees.

Elizabeth relit the extinguished candle with the lit one and sat on the foot of her sister's bed. "What say you to going to the art exhibition on Pall Mall as a viscount's particular companion?"

Kitty's eyes widened. "I would hate the art, but I like the sound of the viscount. Why?"

"Well..." Elizabeth faltered. Now that it came to explaining what had happened earlier that day, she struggled to find the words. It was all too strange. "It is a rather complicated story, but the long and short of it is that I agreed to meet a man there tomorrow—Lord Rutherford. Only I do not want to, and I wondered whether you might go in my place."

"Why do you not want to go?"

"Because I..." *I am in love with somebody else.* "I do not share Mama's eagerness for me to throw myself into the path of rich men."

"You would throw me instead, would you?"

"You cannot tell me you would not enjoy it. Imagine how jealous Lydia would be if your next letter brought the news that you had been keeping company with a viscount." It was crude, but she knew it would work and indeed, Kitty tilted her head and raised her eyebrows in a manner that clearly revealed her interest.

"Why did you agree to meet him in the first place?"

"Because the person who offered to arrange the meeting made it exceedingly difficult to refuse."

Kitty frowned slightly and leant forwards, the bed creaking beneath them. "You are not in trouble, are you?"

"No, not at all," Elizabeth replied with a small huff of laughter. "Well, not really. It is hard to explain. Something very odd happened at the gallery today. Or rather, might have happened—I am not sure, for I did not see it. Somebody may have given me the cut direct."

Kitty lunged to grab Elizabeth's hand and gasped theatrically. "*No!* It was not Mr Knowles, was it? I said you ought not to have refused him!"

"I did not refuse him. Indeed, he has not yet *asked* me anything except whether he may call on me, and I have not said *no* to that."

"You have not said yes, either."

"No, but no man of good sense could ever think that giving me the cut direct in a busy viewing gallery would induce me to do so! Regardless, I did not see who it was. I was not looking."

"Oh." Kitty slumped back against the headboard, sounding terribly disappointed. "Well, what makes you think a slight was intended?"

"I do not. Other people do."

Kitty screwed up her face in confusion.

"I told you it was odd! One minute I was minding my own business, waiting for Aunt Gardiner to catch up, and the next, a stranger appeared at my side, commiserating with me over what had happened, and asking whether I needed her assistance."

"And what *had* happened?"

"According to her, someone walked in, saw me, stared directly at me for long enough for it to be deliberate, then turned around and stormed out again."

"How did you not notice *that*?"

Elizabeth shrugged. "I was not paying attention. There were so many people there, it was sometimes necessary to wait to see the exhibits, so I spent a lot of the time standing about wool-gathering. The only explanation I can think of is that, perhaps, the way I had been staring into space made it *seem* as though we had been looking at each other before whoever it was walked out."

"Then they might just as well have not seen you either."

"Exactly. It was all singularly ridiculous. But this lady—Lady Tuppence Swanbrook, I found out later—was infinitely more concerned by it. She said the cut direct was effectively 'social murder' and insisted on walking me about the room to quell any whispers. Her father is an earl apparently, and she was convinced that would save me by association."

Kitty snorted at the mention of murder. "Why did she care who whispered about you?"

"She said it happened to her once. Someone she thought was a friend cut her at the theatre, and apparently, it caused a stir that lasted an entire Season. She said she could not bear the thought of seeing it happen to someone else."

"Are you sure she was not just prying?" Kitty asked. "I bet she just wanted to find out who you were and why you were given the cut."

"Probably," Elizabeth conceded with a grin, "but even so, she was very kind about it. She insisted on obliging every person she saw pointing at me to talk to us so that none of them could make me a pariah. And she offered to introduce me to her cousin, Lord Rutherford, because she thought that if people saw that he was not afraid to be seen with me, it would stop them gossiping about what happened."

"She offered to introduce her cousin, who is a viscount, to *you*, who is a nobody, for a cut that might not even have been given?"

Elizabeth poked her. "Thank you, but I think I can claim a slightly better social standing than a nobody. And anyhow, by the time she made the offer, we had been talking for a while, and the conversation had turned to what I was doing in London. I made a joke about Mama having sent us here to find husbands."

Kitty scoffed. "Lizzy, you cannot think she meant that her cousin might want to marry you?"

"No, probably not." Elizabeth laughed with her sister, though her mind was instantly crowded with remembrances of another illustrious gentleman declaring himself. "Though, she did seem to think that we might get along. And she joked about it pleasing Mama very well if he did decide he wanted to marry me. But for the most part, she was trying to help me. That is why I felt I had to agree to it. I do not care a whit for what a few strangers in a gallery think of me, but I did not want to appear ungrateful when she was being so kind. Besides, if her family has all the consequence that she seems to think they do, imagine what could happen if she took offence? It would be awful if somebody said something that might affect Uncle Gardiner's business."

"Then you must meet her cousin. It is no use sending me."

"But he only thinks he is meeting a Miss Bennet. He would never know you were the wrong one. He would tell Lady Tuppence the meeting went ahead, and she would assume it was me and not be offended. Please? He is sure to prefer you, anywise. You are far better at flirting. I should only make some careless remark that would offend his pride."

Kitty did not argue—she only narrowed her eyes. "How much does it cost to get into this exhibition? I do not want to spend all my pin money looking at stupid paintings."

"One shilling, which is surely worth the chance to meet a viscount?"

"One shilling is surely worth the cost of me taking your place?"

Elizabeth sighed. "Very well, I shall pay for your ticket to get in. Will you go? It would do your reputation wonders to be seen with such a man. You could drop his name everywhere you go."

"You will have to come with me. Unless I ask my aunt."

"No! I beg you would not mention this to her. She has grown almost as tiresome as Mama when it comes to the subject of men. I shall go with you but stay out of the way while you talk to him. Besides, nobody will be looking at me. They will all be looking at the pretty young girl on Lord Rutherford's arm."

"I shall look a great deal prettier if you allow me to wear your new pelisse and bonnet."

Elizabeth closed her eyes. She had owned the set for less than a week and had thus far managed to keep both from Kitty's greedy clutches. Supposing the amnesty could not have lasted much longer in any case, she sighed in defeat and nodded.

"Very well, I shall do it!" Kitty exclaimed, giving in to a grin which Elizabeth suspected she had been withholding for some time. "It does sound like fun."

It sounded like a recipe for disaster in Elizabeth's opinion, but since it was the only solution she could presently conceive, it would have to do.

CHAPTER FIVE

lizabeth and Kitty returned to the gallery the next day in diametrically opposed states of mind. Kitty was observably bubbling over with anticipation; Elizabeth was on tenterhooks. Several times she had almost resolved to abandon the scheme—it would be better if neither of them went to the gallery and Lady Tuppence and her cousin were allowed to think she had fallen under a carriage on her way there or some such calamity. It was too late, however. Kitty would not hear of crying off now and had gone to great lengths at breakfast to avert all suspicion from Mrs Gardiner as to their intended activity for the day.

"I had no idea it would be this busy," Kitty said once they were inside. "I imagined a few stuffy old men muttering over a couple of easels. If you had told me it was like this, I'd have come with you yesterday. Look how grand everybody is!"

Elizabeth had not known what to expect herself until she stepped through the doors the day before. The entire exhibition was like nothing she had ever seen. There was scarcely an inch of wall showing between all the frames that hung from floor to ceiling in every room. Tables and easels displaying yet more paintings were arranged in clusters wherever there was a patch of floor large enough. She suspected, however, that the exhibits that were of greatest interest were the people themselves.

Ladies and gentlemen glided about with exaggerated state, chins held high, chests thrust forward, and wealth announced by every stitch of their fashionable clothes. The British Institution on Pall Mall was apparently the place to be and be seen this Season. Elizabeth hoped that meant nobody would notice her, for she had deliberately worn her plainest walking dress and intended to loiter about the least popular displays until her sister was done.

"How shall I know him?" Kitty enquired as they made their way up the stairs.

"I suppose he will introduce himself."

"Is that not terribly improper?"

"Yes, but I gather it was Lady Tuppence's intention to make it seem as though he and I were already acquainted. She hoped his consequence would trump my disgrace— such as she viewed it."

"Should I act as though I know him then?"

A frisson of alarm made Elizabeth regret again embroiling her impressionable younger sister in such a foolhardy arrangement. "Do not be over familiar. You would not like to give him any notions. And I shall remain within sight at all times. If you feel uneasy at *any* point, you must simply come to me, do you understand?"

"If you say so, Lizzy. Look at that lady's spencer! Ooh, I would *die* for one like it!"

Elizabeth sighed and directed her sister through first one, then another large chamber, towards the designated meeting point. "There is the couch, at the far end. I believe we are a little early, though. Shall we walk about a bit while we wait—look at some of the exhibits?"

Kitty wrinkled her nose. "I would rather poke my eyes out. I shall wait sitting down, thank you." So saying, she darted between the people in front of them and plonked herself down on the couch so inelegantly that she bounced once or twice before coming to rest.

Elizabeth moved to the side of the room, positioning herself between two larger groups and trying her best to be inconspicuous. Her first two glances at the couch showed her sister still waiting patiently for Lord Rutherford. Her view was momentarily obstructed when a large group sauntered by, but her next glance revealed Kitty still alone and growing fidgety, chewing her lip and drumming her fingers on her knees.

An outburst of unladylike sniggering made Elizabeth and several other people turn around to look at the perpetrators—two women, both certainly old enough to know better. One of them caught Elizabeth's eye, stopped laughing, and turned quickly away. Trying to quell a gnawing suspicion, Elizabeth turned back to the wall to feign interest in the array of corpulent, scantily clad, and generally flaccid bodies displayed there.

She could not long resist the temptation to glance over her shoulder again and was taken aback when she was met with the direct gaze of the man and woman behind her. They averted their eyes immediately, but Elizabeth still frowned over it. Surely Lady Tuppence had not been correct—*surely* nobody here remembered her or her imagined cut? She sighed irritably. She ought to have known a place which attracted so much that was fashionable would also attract a good deal that was vacuous.

Moving to stand in front of an easel with a still life propped upon it, she watched surreptitiously to see whether the crowd's attention would follow her there, but it was impossible to tell without looking at people directly. She raised her eyes but entirely forgot to take note of who was looking at her when her gaze fell on the couch. It was empty, and her sister was nowhere to be seen.

She turned her head this way and that, searching the room for her own pink pelisse that Kitty had been so desperate to wear, but could see no sign of either. Her efforts to force her way through the crowds drew grumbles, and she felt certain this must be the best way possible of guaranteeing an increase in unwanted notice. Gritting her teeth, she held her head high and walked as calmly as she could to the next room. There, with as much urgency as she could manage without drawing further attention to herself, she began weaving in and out of the crush in search of her sister.

Real alarm did not assert itself until Elizabeth had searched every corner of every room of the gallery to no avail. A rare moment of irrationality beset her as she dreamt up all manner of unthinkable misfortunes that might have befallen Kitty. She berated herself for ever having been fool enough to suggest a meeting with a stranger. After a deep breath to collect herself, she reasoned that a second search of the exhibition rooms ought probably to be conducted before she gave way to complete panic, and she set out back the way she had come.

The nearer she drew to the first room, the greater her dread became that she would walk back in to find everybody staring at her. She wished Lady Tuppence had not put the notion in her head. The scorn of a few strangers would not usually give her any concern whatsoever, yet here she was, panicking at every passing glance that might be meant for her. By the time she caught a brief glimpse of two people on the couch, one dressed in pink, her relief was almost entirely offset by exasperation.

She hastened through the ever-shifting sea of visitors to fetch Kitty and tell her she wished to leave that instant. Only, just as she came within ten feet of the couch, she heard her sister laugh, somewhere off to her left. She craned her neck to look, and there was Kitty, on the arm of a dark-haired man in a scarlet coat. Not just any scarlet coat, either—regimentals.

She did not wonder that her sister was happy, in that case, but she frowned over it, nevertheless. She could not recall that Lady Tuppence had mentioned the viscount being an officer. Indeed, it would be most unusual if he were, although, she supposed, not unheard of. Regardless, she supposed she ought not to whisk Kitty away too quickly, for her sister did so admire a soldier. She turned back to the couch, hoping there might be space next to whomever she had seen sitting there, that she might wait in comfort. She almost squealed when the people milling in front of her moved out of the way and revealed the lady in pink to be Mr Darcy's sister.

CHAPTER SIX

With a quick, sideways pirouette, Elizabeth ducked into the nearest hiding place—the empty space behind a large pillar to one side of the couch—and there found sweet sanctuary. A private area, out of sight, with just enough room to lean against the cool exterior wall while she collected herself. A space where she could—and presently did—laugh silently but heartily at her own ridiculous compulsion.

Miss Darcy was one of the gentlest, most mild-mannered young ladies Elizabeth had ever met; to hide from her was wholly unnecessary, she was sure. Yet, they had not been in company since the previous summer at Pemberley, and any conversation was likely to include news of her brother's comings and goings in the intervening months—his inevitable preference for some new lady, perhaps even his marriage. Considering which, Elizabeth did not blame whatever part of herself had decided to bolt like a startled animal upon seeing her.

She had long ago acknowledged that Mr Darcy would eventually marry someone else, but she could not say that she was yet reconciled to the idea. It made her feel rather bilious, in fact. Although good sense told her one must exist, *she* could not imagine another woman who, in disposition and talents, would suit him as well as she. A woman of the same unbending and fastidious temperament as Mr Darcy would not do at all! He needed liveliness such as hers to improve his manners and soften his heart. She fancied there were few, if any, women of his acquaintance willing to be sportive with him in the way she was.

Stupid girl! she chided herself. Patently, it was not liveliness Mr Darcy wanted, otherwise he would have come back.

She sighed heavily in an attempt to dispel the disagreeable reverie—and when that did not work, she leant to peer carefully around the pillar to determine how easily she might slip away without being noticed by the pair on the couch. Miss Darcy and her gentleman friend appeared to be deep in conversation about the exhibition. *The only people in the entire place genuinely interested in the paintings,* Elizabeth mused.

"It never occurred to me to consider it in such a way," Miss Darcy was saying. "It would be wonderful to hear more, but I must go. My companion and I have another engagement this afternoon."

"What a shame," the gentleman replied.

"It truly is. I declare, I could come here every day and always find something new to appreciate."

"Then, what do you say to doing just that?"

"My lord?"

"Pardon me—I recognise that our acquaintance is of exceedingly short duration, but I have enjoyed it enormously. I wondered whether you would consent to meeting me back here again tomorrow, at the same time. I shall tell you everything I know about whichever paintings you choose."

Elizabeth felt her cheeks flush with heat, mortified to have trespassed on such an intimate discussion. If she knew her at all, she imagined Miss Darcy must also be blushing fiercely in the face of such marked attention.

"I should like that very well indeed," Miss Darcy replied, and her breathless voice did indeed reveal all the awkwardness of overt flattery.

"Excellent," the gentleman said. Elizabeth jerked backwards to avoid being seen as he began to stand up, thus she could not see him as he said, "Until noon tomorrow, madam."

Neither could she see Miss Darcy as she replied, "Until noon tomorrow, Lord Rutherford."

Then, despite all her efforts to remain out of sight, Elizabeth could not help but thrust her head around the pillar to gape at the pair in disbelief, but they were already walking away. She came out from her hiding place and stared after them, confused and not a little alarmed. If that was Lord Rutherford, to whose arm was Kitty clinging?

"There you are, Lizzy! Where have you been?"

She looked around to see Kitty emerge from the same churning crush in the centre of the room into which Miss Darcy and Lord Rutherford had just disappeared. "Where have I been? Where were *you*? I looked everywhere!"

"I was taking in the exhibition. Most of the portraits are nudes, you know!"

With a last, infuriated groan, Elizabeth grabbed Kitty's elbow and directed her firmly around the outside of the room towards the exit. Under her breath, she whispered, "Who were you talking to? I know it was not Lord Rutherford."

"No—and thank goodness it was not! Would you cease shoving me? What is the rush?"

"What do you mean 'thank goodness it was not Lord Rutherford'?"

Kitty jerked her arm out of Elizabeth's grip and made a great show of rubbing it. "Apparently, he is an awful man. You brought me to meet a rake."

No less confused than appalled, Elizabeth stopped walking, but before she could think what to say, Kitty pointed at her and said, "I told you you should have worn a different gown."

"What?"

"Have you not noticed the way everybody is looking at it? Honestly, what were you thinking? You came here on Monday—you must have known this place was little more than a walking fashion plate, yet you still came dressed as a milkmaid."

A quick look around confirmed it. People *were* staring, but not at her. It seemed her vastly unfashionable gown had been the cause of every sidelong sneer. She shook her head in consternation and tugged Kitty towards the door. "Rest assured I shall not wear it here a second time, for I believe I may safely promise you *never* to come back to this place again."

Elizabeth thanked the attendants at the door and bustled Kitty out, setting off directly for home. "Tell me everything. Who was that man and what did he say to you about Lord Rutherford?" She did not miss the look that crossed her sister's face as she began her explanation—a faraway aspect in her eyes and a dreamy smile.

"His name is Sergeant Mulhall. When he sat down next to me, I thought he must be Lord Rutherford, so I did not hesitate to talk to him. He told me he came to see the paintings but was not much taken with any of them and that he was only sitting on the couch to get his full shilling's worth before leaving again."

Elizabeth gritted her teeth and schooled herself to patience, certain that hastening her sister would only dissuade her from telling the story at all. She nevertheless wished Kitty would spare her the minutiae.

"We spoke a bit about how pointless most of the paintings were—who wants to look at pictures of flowers and hay wains when you can just as easily go outside and look at the real thing? And he asked me why I had come if I did not like art." She giggled. "That was when I realised he was not Lord Rutherford, because when I said I was there to meet him, he said he was very glad to have made my acquaintance, but he had no idea who I was."

"At which point, he presumed to introduce himself, did he?"

"Well, we had already been talking, so I thought I might as well allow it."

Elizabeth sighed quietly. She supposed it was no more inappropriate than the meeting that had been supposed to take place.

"In any case, he asked me who I thought he was, and when I said 'Lord Rutherford,' he went all peculiar."

"In what way?"

"Sort of...stiff. Like Mary goes when you say something rude, and she disapproves but doesn't want to say so. I had to work on him for quite a while before he admitted that he had heard of the viscount. He was quite reluctant to tell me anything, but I could tell he was concerned, so I refused to give up."

"Poor man," Elizabeth remarked wryly. Kitty could be relentless when she had set her mind to something.

"But I made him tell me in the end. According to him, Lord Rutherford is shockingly loose in the haft, and not to be trusted with any woman's virtue."

Elizabeth frowned doubtfully. She had learnt the hard way that giving credit to the slanderous whispers of strangers was a guaranteed way of making trouble for oneself. It was on the basis of Wickham's lies that she had rejected the only man she had ever met who she truly believed could make her happy. The present situation differed somewhat, for she knew neither Lord Rutherford nor this sergeant Mulhall—it ought not to matter what either man thought of the other. Except there was now another party involved, and it mattered very much to Elizabeth that she not be caught up in any unpleasantness.

"Did he say how he knew Lord Rutherford?"

Kitty squinted at nothing, then shook her head. "I cannot remember."

"It makes no sense. Why would Lady Tuppence think it helpful to my reputation to be seen with a man of dubious honour?"

Her sister shrugged. "Maybe she does not know her cousin is a cad. Bad people rarely go about shouting their wickedness from the rooftops. Either way, I am not sorry. Sergeant Mulhall was a most agreeable substitute. He is so witty! I thought I might pee myself when he told me he had counted thirty-four bare bottoms in that first room alone."

"Faith, Kitty! I beg you would exercise *some* decorum. You are nearly nineteen years old and hoping to secure a husband. No man of worth has ever been captivated by vulgar manners or a propensity to laugh oneself to incontinence at the slightest inanity."

"Sergeant Mulhall enjoyed it well enough when I laughed."

Elizabeth refrained from sighing at her sister's naivety. "Good for him. Is he planning on marrying you?"

"Maybe. He has asked me to meet him for a walk in Potters Fields tomorrow."

"What?" Elizabeth looked at her sharply. Her sister still wore the same wistful expression. "Kitty, you cannot do that. You do not know him."

All the softness fell away from Kitty's face. "I did not know Lord Rutherford, but you left me to meet him alone —and it turns out he is an out-and-out reprobate!"

"I did not leave you alone. At least, I did not intend to." She stopped making excuses and blew out her cheeks in surrender. "You are right. I ought never to have agreed to meet Lord Rutherford, and I certainly should not have asked you to meet him in my stead. I am very sorry. But even more reason not to do it again—especially not outdoors, away from the safety of other people. It is entirely unsuitable."

"But if you came with me, it would be respectable. There is no rule that says two sisters cannot walk in a park and say good day if they happen to see an acquaintance."

"He is not an acquaintance. And there *is* a rule—it says, 'Lizzy Bennet has no wish to walk in Potters Fields'."

"But you like walking."

"Not there, and not tomorrow."

Kitty, whose strides had been increasing in length and pace the angrier she grew, now stopped walking altogether and regarded Elizabeth with her jaw set. "You will not go with me? Despite what I did for you today?"

"I will not go with you because it is not a good idea. If he likes you, let him call on you."

"He does not know where I live."

"That is because he is not a proper acquaintance."

"But I really like him."

"Very well. If you are so determined it is a good idea, ask Aunt Gardiner to accompany you."

Kitty growled in frustration. "You know she would never agree to it!"

"That is your answer, then."

"I cannot believe you!" Kitty stormed off again, her boots banging audibly on the pavement and her angry words half swallowed up by the wind. "You are an absolute...have it your way...not go...*hate* you!"

They walked the whole way back to Gracechurch Street fifteen yards removed from each other, and Kitty went directly to their room as soon as they arrived home. Elizabeth felt terrible, and not just for refusing her help. She must take responsibility for having almost introduced her sister to a libertine as well. Yet, no matter how passionately Kitty had pleaded for her chaperonage the next day, she could not have agreed to it. She had a different engagement to intercept.

CHAPTER SEVEN

Georgiana was in better spirits than she had known for many months. Never could she have imagined that an encounter of but a few moments with a complete stranger could induce such an enduring sense of happiness, yet here she was, hours after her brief exchange with Lord Rutherford, still aglow with pleasure. She harboured a small measure of guilt for not yet mentioning the meeting to anybody, but she would, when a suitable opportunity arose.

Her companion would be the trickiest to handle. Mrs Annesley had been hired after the debacle in Ramsgate, when Georgiana had narrowly escaped ruin at the hands of George Wickham. She was a kind lady, but so determined to fulfil her role as protector that Georgiana had only to look at a member of the opposite sex to receive a stern reminder of the fragility of women's virtue and be dragged away to safety. That would be well and good if she were still a naive fifteen-year-old. As it was, she was only a few months shy of eighteen and was in London for her first Season. If the whole object was not to meet men, then she knew not what it was.

Her brother and cousin might be more reasonable, for they were desirous of her making a suitable match, and Lord Rutherford was assuredly no Wickham. He was, perhaps, a little less handsome, but where the latter's countenance was permanently decorated with the easy grins of shameless flirtation, the former's was more nobly framed with the genuine smiles of quiet respect. Moreover, Lord Rutherford was a viscount; he was courteous and well-informed—and steadfastly proper, for he had asked repeatedly for an introduction to Mrs Annesley and was only denied one because Georgiana had pretended not to be able to see her in the crowds and begged to defer one until the morrow. For now, she held her secret close, revelling in the anticipation of seeing him again the next day, and wondering what had occurred to put everybody else in such ill humour.

Her cousin Fitzwilliam had come to dine with them, but unlike the usual banter and cajolery he brought with him, there had persisted a strange tension to both his and Darcy's demeanours throughout dinner. It reminded Georgiana, disagreeably, of their comportment shortly after her failed elopement. They each had that same restless look about them, exchanging furtive glances and seeming impatient for her to be gone so that they might talk about her.

Strongly averse to giving them any such opportunity,

she asked them to forgo their after-dinner brandies and join her directly in the drawing room. Mrs Annesley's absence due to a prior engagement gave convenient credence to her plea not to be left alone, and Darcy and the colonel dutifully followed her out of the dining room.

Ten minutes later, she rather regretted not simply going to bed and leaving them to say whatever they liked about her. Her brother had taken up a position leaning against the mantel, staring blankly into the empty hearth, and occasionally nudging the grate with the toe of his boot. The colonel seemed to be on a mission to drink the house dry of spirits and had already made three trips to the sideboard to refill his glass. Neither seemed inclined to speak.

With a sigh, Georgiana comprehended that if she wished for conversation, she would have to start one herself. The pall in the room was certainly not conducive to broaching the subject of Lord Rutherford, but thinking of that reminded her of something else she thought might lighten the mood. She wished she had thought of it earlier.

"I saw your batman at the gallery on Pall Mall today, Cousin. With a young lady. He was being terribly sweet, pointing out all the finest paintings to her. I may have inadvertently-on-purpose stood close enough to hear him invite her to walk out with him tomorrow in Potters Fields."

She had been expecting this to draw some amusement, at least from the colonel, if not her brother. Instead, it brought Darcy whipping around to face them, his expression one of furious disbelief, while the colonel raised both eyebrows in a guilty fashion and took a vast gulp of his drink.

"Is that not romantic of him?" she added, all bewilderment.

Both men ignored her. Darcy took two angry strides towards Fitzwilliam then drew up short and pressed a fist to his lips. After several measured inhalations through his nose, he said, "You sent *Mulhall* to meet Elizabeth?"

This did nothing to lessen Georgiana's confusion. "Elizabeth...Bennet? No, Brother, it was not her. At least, I do not think it was. Although, I was behind them, so I cannot be absolutely certain." Upon reflection, the young woman had been wearing a pelisse of a similar colour to the one Georgiana had last seen Miss Bennet wearing. And she was of a similar height. And she had spoken in similar accents. "Actually...it could have been her. I wish I had known. I would have said good day. I ought to have said *something*. Perhaps." The more she said, the more darkly her brother scowled. "Or perhaps not."

"What were you doing at the gallery? I thought you had already been," Fitzwilliam asked her. He looked at her intently as he awaited her answer. Georgiana thought it an excessively flimsy ploy to avoid Darcy's ferocious glare.

"I did not have the opportunity to take in the whole exhibition on my first visit. Indeed, I might go again tomorrow, for there are so many fine works there, I believe I could go every day for a month and find something new to see every time."

That was not untrue—the skill of the artists and intricacy of the art fascinated her—though she thought that day's particular find would be difficult to best. When Lord Rutherford had sat down next to her with his unaffected, affable smile, her heart had leapt about like a jack-in-the-box. When he began to talk, openly and warmly, as though they were old acquaintances, she had quite melted with delight. It had not been long, of course, before his mistake came to light—she was not the individual his cousin had sent him to meet. That young lady had never appeared, however, and instead, Lord Rutherford had enraptured Georgiana with his knowledge of the paintings and their various artists. She grew warm remembering his gentle but sincere attentiveness and dared to wonder whether he was thinking of her with the same fondness.

"At a shilling a visit, you would do better to look more diligently the first time," Fitzwilliam quipped.

Nobody laughed. His smile died on his lips. Darcy continued to glare rancorously at him. Georgiana decided it would be a spectacularly impolitic moment to mention her assignation with Lord Rutherford, and excused herself to bed without reference to him, her plans for the morrow, or the unfamiliar but not unpleasant flutter of anticipation in her stomach.

———•———

The door closed, and Darcy rounded on his cousin. "*Mulhall?* Hell's bells, Fitzwilliam, I thought you comprehended how important this was to me!"

His cousin held up one hand in defence and used the other to push himself from his chair. "Untwist your bollocks, man. Something came up at the barracks, and I could not get away. It was send Mulhall or leave her to Rutherford, and I knew you would not like me to do that." He approached and grasped Darcy's shoulder. "He assured me the message was safely delivered and your part in it kept concealed."

Darcy batted his hand away and walked with quick steps across the room. He had been waiting all evening with barely repressed impatience to hear it confirmed that Elizabeth had been forewarned, that she was safe. Beyond that, he had grown nigh on desperate to hear news of her, to have her words relayed to him—to discover whether she had asked after him. It was a chance—and one that was never likely to be repeated—to have some small connexion to her, however fleeting, and this alteration blasted his last hopes of achieving even that much.

"Yes!" he retorted. "He warned her off Rutherford, then jumped directly into his place! What the devil? Elizabeth *cannot* step out with your batman! I will not see her saved from one blackguard only to be passed around the bloody barracks!"

"Steady on," Fitzwilliam replied defensively. "Mulhall is a decent fellow. In fact, if you cease your paroxysms for a moment and look at it with an impartial eye, he is not a bad match for her."

"An *impartial eye*? Is that supposed to be amusing?"

"No—unusually. Look, he is from a good family, he is

not without connexions—yours truly included. He has money, and he is a thoroughly nice chap. He is also not a cad. Miss Bennet could do a lot worse."

"She could also do a darn sight better! Fitzwilliam, *you* may be easy watching the man who irons your shirts make love to the woman I want to be my wife, but I assure you, I am not!"

Fitzwilliam had filled two glasses while Darcy railed, and he came towards him now with one proffered in a conciliatory gesture. "Forgive me. I have, once again, underestimated the strength of your regard for Miss Bennet. You must give some allowance for the fact that this old dog has a very confined *modus operandi* when it comes to the fairer sex. I am afraid sensibility is outside my area of expertise."

Darcy accepted the glass and knocked back a substantial gulp before conceding, with a sardonic huff of laughter, "As it is mine."

Fitzwilliam dropped back into his chair. "I shall speak to Mulhall. Tell him not to meet her." He must have perceived Darcy's dissatisfaction, for he added, with an impatient sigh, "Will that not suffice? What troubles you now?"

"I cannot like the thought of her left wandering the park, waiting in vain for him to come. In Potters Fields, too! Hardly the sort of place a young lady ought to loiter if she can avoid it. What was Mulhall thinking?"

"Who says it was his idea? It is not far from the City— perhaps she suggested it. Not everybody has the means to hop in a curricle and trot all the way across town to prance up and down Rotten Row at the drop of a hat. But in any case, I daresay she is not foolish enough to go alone."

Darcy grimaced, all too aware of Elizabeth's propensity to walk unaccompanied, sometimes for many miles.

Fitzwilliam let out an almighty sigh. "Very well! I shall go myself and explain to Miss Bennet that Mulhall cannot be spared from his duties. But I beg you would make this the last time I must interfere in your disastrous love life."

It was on the tip of Darcy's tongue to remind Fitzwilliam of the damage he had already done to his love life by the careless disclosure to Elizabeth of his part in separating Bingley and her sister. Were it not for that, Darcy's proposal might not have been so emphatically rejected, and his efforts to win back Elizabeth's good opinion might have met with more success.

He said nothing of it. The past could not be changed, and he needed Fitzwilliam to help avoid a future disaster. He only thanked him and prayed no further incidents would occur at the barracks that would prevent him going this time.

CHAPTER EIGHT

"What are you doing tomorrow?" Elizabeth asked quietly.

She was not entirely sure that her aunt heard the question. The candles were burning low, Kitty had long since gone up to bed, and Mr Gardiner was still in the dining parlour, demolishing his finest bottle of port with the two men of business who had come for dinner. Mrs Gardiner, too polite to retire to her own bed until her husband's guests departed, had grown sleepy, her head lolling against the wing of her chair and her eyes closed more often than they were open. She spoke eventually but mumbled her answer and kept her eyes closed.

"I have no fixed engagements. Why do you ask?"

"I was wondering whether you might accompany me to the British Institution again."

Mrs Gardiner did not move other than to open her eyes and squint doubtfully. "You surprise me, Lizzy. It was a fine exhibition, but you gave no hint of having enjoyed it so well."

"I am sorry if I gave that impression. You were very good to take me, and I liked it very much, truly. But I shall not lie—it is not the exhibition I wish to see this time."

The look on her aunt's face as she came fully alert and sat up in her chair was everything Elizabeth had wished to avoid, but there had been no choice but to ask her to act as chaperon. Appealing to Kitty had been pointless after their quarrel; Annie, the maid, had said she had other business the next day and was not available to help; and Pall Mall was too far, and the gallery too full of propriety-conscious busybodies for Elizabeth to go alone. This was her last resort, and it had taken until almost midnight to drum up the courage to broach the matter.

"Out with it, then," Mrs Gardiner said warily. "What is it you wish to see?"

"'Tis not what but whom. Miss Darcy will be there tomorrow. I would like to speak to her."

Her aunt gave a quiet groan and shook her head. "Lizzy, this has to stop. You cannot continue to—"

"Pray, allow me to explain. This has nothing to do with Mr Darcy. At least, not in the way you are imagining. I am well aware *that* situation is hopeless, and I assure you, this is not some indelicate scheme to renew the acquaintance. Indeed, I am hopeful that he will never find out I have spoken to his sister."

"You do not think it likely Miss Darcy would tell him?"

"No. In fact, I believe the subject I wish to speak of is

one she would vastly prefer to keep him from finding out about at all costs."

"You have something specific to say to her, then? I assumed you only wished to say 'how do you do'." She waved the matter away and slid to the edge of her seat. "You had better tell me what this is about."

Elizabeth knew she must tread a careful path between deception and truth, undesirous of trespassing upon either. She had meant it when she said she did not wish to lie to her aunt; nevertheless, it was surely not necessary to disclose every detail. Vagueness seemed the safest course to take. Thus, she began by explaining that she and Kitty had returned to the gallery without elaborating as to why.

Mrs Gardiner seemed not to notice the omission. "Now I comprehend her high dudgeon this evening. Your sister has never been much of a one for the arts."

Elizabeth did not contradict her and went on, instead, to explain her cowardly lunge for cover upon seeing Miss Darcy, as well as her subsequent overhearings.

"I take it, from your expression, that this troubles you," her aunt replied, "but I cannot see that anything overly worrying occurred. Their introduction was a little improper, to be sure, but if Miss Darcy wishes to see the gentleman again, it is no business of ours."

"I would agree with you entirely if Lord Rutherford were a man of honour."

"Have you reason to think he is not?"

"Unfortunately, yes. There was talk about him at the gallery. Kitty heard him referred to as a rake."

Her aunt regarded her expectantly for a moment, before asking in a disapproving tone, "Was that it?"

Elizabeth shifted on her seat, uncomfortable to be sailing so close to disguise. "No. I also understand, from what I heard myself, that he was at the gallery to meet a different lady but threw her over as soon as he set eyes on Miss Darcy. It cannot speak well of his character that he was willing to disappoint one young lady the moment another took his fancy."

"Lizzy, this is meaningless gossip—a few spurious remarks overheard in a busy gallery. You ought to know better than to pay attention to such things."

"And in the usual course of things, I would think nothing of it. But I have another reason to be concerned."

"Oh?"

Elizabeth sighed heavily. "I would not, under any other circumstance, reveal this, for my discretion in this matter has been as valuable to Mr Darcy as his was to us when it came to Lydia's elopement."

Mrs Gardiner frowned deeply and assured Elizabeth that she could depend upon her secrecy. She and her husband, Elizabeth knew, thought exceptionally well of Mr Darcy for the probity and generosity he had shown in saving Lydia from ruin. They had assumed, at the time, he had done it for their niece. That it had not turned out to be affection which motivated him, whilst it made them sorry for her, had only increased their good opinion of him. For if it had not been love that induced him, it could only have been the finest sense of honour.

"Lydia was not the first girl whom Wickham almost ruined," Elizabeth whispered, as though saying it aloud might be ruinous despite there being nobody else present to hear. "Before her, he persuaded Miss Darcy to believe herself in love with him. She was but fifteen at the time. Their elopement was only prevented because Mr Darcy visited his sister unexpectedly, and she confessed the whole of it to him."

Her aunt pursed her lips and exhaled heavily through her nose. "Your new brother has a lot to answer for. No wonder Mr Darcy was so reluctant to reveal his true character to the world—his poor sister!"

"Exactly. Do you see now why I am fearful for her? She has been burnt once before, almost irreparably. She is such a dear, sweet girl—so shy and trusting. I would warn her to be careful of Lord Rutherford, that is all. I cannot bear the thought of her being ill-used again."

"It would be a tragedy, I agree, but it is not our place to intervene, and certainly not on the grounds of two unsubstantiated rumours. You would do better to have your uncle send a note to Mr Darcy. Let her brother be the one to investigate the matter."

Elizabeth shook her head—and rather more violently than she intended to, but that was the solution she was *least* inclined to pursue. "You have not heard from him since Lydia's wedding. That can mean only one thing—that he did not wish to maintain an acquaintance with you, any more than he did with me. And really, who can blame him, for we are now related to a man he justly scorns."

"True, but in these circumstances, a simple letter would surely present no evil."

"But it would! Imagine, the first contact in months from a family he would sooner forget, and it is with the accusation that his sister is engaged in another illicit liaison! Censure all the more problematic precisely because, as you say, the reports are unsubstantiated." She shook her head again. "I cannot hurl any more unfounded charges at Mr Darcy; it would be unthinkably cruel—not to mention unfair to his sister and mortifying for me. It would be much better if I were to have a quiet word with Miss Darcy at the gallery. Mr Darcy need never know."

The answer was going to be no; Elizabeth could tell. Her aunt's mien was sympathetic, but she was taking a long time to answer, and that meant she was preparing her excuses. "I shall never have the chance to thank him for what he did for Lydia," she interjected before Mrs Gardiner could speak. "If I can do this one thing, if I can protect his sister, it would be the closest to repaying him I shall ever have the opportunity for."

She saw the indecision in her aunt's countenance—and she saw it disappear again when the door opened, and her uncle poked his head into the room.

"Gregg and Sawyer are leaving, my dear."

Mrs Gardiner hastened to her feet, urgently seeking assurances that neither of the gentlemen wished for coffee.

"Gregg has an early appointment," Mr Gardiner explained, holding the door open for his wife. He seemed surprised when Elizabeth stood up to follow them both into the hall. "Lizzy! I thought you went to bed when your sister did. You are good to stay up and keep your aunt company."

"Not at all, Uncle, it was my pleasure." She followed him along the passage to the entrance hall, where Mr Sawyer and Mr Gregg were shrugging into their coats in readiness to leave. She tried her best to be cheerful as she wished them both farewell, but privately, she could think of little other than how awful it would be if, after everything Mr Darcy had done for her sister, her inaction allowed *his* sister to come to harm.

"You *are* good, Lizzy. You have a big heart," her aunt whispered, startling her. She looked up and was greeted with a kind smile and kinder words. "I shall go with you tomorrow. It will be pleasant to see Miss Darcy again. She is a sweet girl."

The magnitude of her relief made even Elizabeth begin to doubt her earlier avowals of being reconciled to her acquaintance with Mr Darcy being over, but there was nothing she could do about that. She might see him again, or she might not; for now, Miss Darcy would be warned, and Mr Darcy would be spared the pain of seeing his sister unhappy again. That was all that mattered. She thanked her aunt in the warmest of terms and excused herself to bed.

CHAPTER NINE

K itty refused her sister and aunt's invitation to return to the gallery again the next morning. She made her refusal in as sulky a way as she possibly could to ensure that neither pressed the point. Then she lingered over her breakfast, dawdled over her toilette, and generally made it seem as though leaving the house was the least agreeable prospect in the world. It worked; they departed for the gallery without her, leaving behind them the counsel that she ought to find something to do while they were out that would put her in a better humour.

They need not have concerned themselves; Kitty had plans that would raise any girl's spirits—and since her ill temper was entirely fictitious in any case, her humour looked set to become positively jubilant before too long. As soon as she heard the front door close, she abandoned her magazine, snatched up her bonnet and cloak, and hastened to the back of the house, where she knew Annie awaited her.

"They have gone! Time to go!"

The maid finished folding the napkin in her hands and set it on a pile of others, then picked up her own pelisse and bonnet from the chair beside her. "'Tis a relief, miss, I don't mind admitting. I had a hard time hiding from your sister all morning."

"Why were you hiding from Lizzy?"

"She asked me to go with her today. I had to tell her I had other plans, since you asked me not to let on about ours, only then I had to keep out of her way, and I thought she would discover me at every minute."

Kitty grinned and gave an affected sigh of relief. She had originally planned to feign a headache and sneak out of the house to keep her meeting with Sergeant Mulhall while everybody else thought she was resting. She had secured Annie's services as a chaperon for the venture the moment she returned from her outing with Lizzy the previous day. It was a feeble plan, almost certain to be foiled—not least because she shared a bedroom with her sister, and the chances of her absence from it going undiscovered were therefore vanishingly small. She had scarcely believed her luck when Lizzy and Mrs Gardiner announced their intention to go out, leaving her at liberty to come and go as she pleased without disguise.

"Well done for not getting caught—but what a fine adventure!" she cried. Ignoring Annie's muted enthusiasm, she led the way out of the back door. "We had better make haste—'tis almost noon already, and I do not want to be late."

They made their way towards the river, where they crossed the bridge into Southwark and turned eastwards. It was a warm day, and Kitty regretted wearing her cloak, but she refrained from asking Annie to take it, for she was in a far worse state, short of breath and gleaming with exertion —clearly unfit to be burdened with anything to carry. She wondered whether the maid was unused to walking so far, but she ought to be glad to have come with her, in that case, for if she had gone with Lizzy, she would have had to walk twice as far at twice the pace.

After half an hour they were both flushed from the midday heat and fed up with standing about in it. The park —if it could be called that, for it was little more than a stretch of common land in the midst of a tract of dilapidated factories—was teeming with people. Some led horse-drawn carts loaded with goods, others pulled small children along by the hand. The odd few clung wearily to the leading rope of a grazing goat or sheep. It was assuredly not Hyde Park: nobody was there to take the air, which was acrid with smoke and the ever-present tang of sewage from the nearby river; everybody but them was passing through, seemingly with as much haste as they could.

"We might as well have met at Rotten Row. We could have walked to Hyde Park and back in the time we have been waiting here."

Annie nodded glumly and shivered.

"You cannot possibly be cold," Kitty said irritably.

"I'm not, miss. 'Tis the thought of all those bodies."

"What bodies?"

The maid pointed at the ground. "They used to bury people here."

Kitty was more unnerved by this than she wished to be but having already observed that nobody seemed keen to hang about, she felt suddenly anxious that they might know something she did not. She shrugged defiantly. "They bury people in a lot of places."

Annie may have had a response to this, but it was lost to a yelp of fright when a sudden commotion broke out nearby. A dog barked, a child wailed, several people shouted, and a sheep, frightened out of its owner's grip and bleating manically, came charging through the long grass towards them. Annie turned tail and ran. Kitty would have done likewise, but the sheep bashed against her as it barrelled past, knocking her to the ground.

As she lay on her back, staring at the sky, thinking unkind thoughts about her sister for dragging her to the stupid gallery and embroiling her in this whole fiasco in the first place, a face appeared above her.

"May I assist you, madam?"

It was a man, and when he held out his arm, Kitty saw that it was sleeved in scarlet red. That drew her attention to the decorations adorning his breast, and she smiled to herself. Sergeant Mulhall had been well and truly outranked. "Thank you, sir. You are very kind."

Strong arms pulled her up and set her on her feet. "Are you hurt?"

"I do not think so." She began to brush herself off. "Only embarrassed."

"It is not you who ought to be embarrassed, but that oaf, for letting his livestock run amok." The officer pointed to where an elderly gentleman was unsuccessfully attempting to recapture his highly intractable sheep. Not far from him, taking a wide berth around the animal, Annie was making her way back towards them. "That is your companion?" the man enquired.

Kitty confirmed that it was.

"Well and good. If you had been on your own, I would have offered to escort you home, but as it is, I have other business, so your having a friend to accompany you is most advantageous."

"I suppose I might as well go home. I was supposed to be meeting somebody, but he evidently decided he had better things to do, for he has not come." She stopped speaking, for Annie had arrived back and begun fussing at her gown, tutting and shaking her head at the streaks of dust and mud.

"A thousand apologies, Miss Bennet! I ought never to have abandoned you like that."

"It is well, Annie, stop fretting." To the officer, Kitty said, "He was a soldier, too—perhaps you know him?"

The officer was looking at her most peculiarly. "Perhaps I do. Pray, what is his name?"

"Sergeant Mulhall."

It was immediately apparent that the two men *were* acquainted, for a look of comprehension came over the officer's countenance, and he grimaced as though realising a mistake. "Ah...in that case, I believe I owe you an apology, madam. Sergeant Mulhall is, in fact, my batman. And I am happy to report that he has not deliberately disappointed you. I had an urgent errand that needed running, and I am afraid I gave him no choice but to see to it this very morning. The fault for his desertion is mine entirely."

"Oh, I see," Kitty replied, still disheartened, for the officer's gallant acknowledgement of blame in no way relieved her disappointment. "What a strange coincidence that I have met you in the same place."

"Ah...no. No, not really. Not at all, in fact, for the errand was in a place not far from here. Indeed, I was just on my way to join him."

"I see. Good day then, sir. Come, Annie. It seems there is no point in us waiting here any longer." Kitty curtseyed and turned to leave, but the officer forestalled her.

"I, ah...I do recall him mentioning, though, that he had met a very lovely young lady at the gallery yesterday."

She blushed with pleasure, despite her dissatisfaction. "That was me."

"Well then, he spoke true—you are, indeed, *quite* lovely. I see now why he was so angry to be commissioned elsewhere this morning. I am sorry for it. Allow me to make amends. What say I tell him to meet you again tomorrow? At the exhibition, at noon."

Kitty let out a little huff of laughter before she could help herself. "Another chance to see him would be most welcome, but if it is all the same, I should prefer a different meeting place. The whole world and his dog are at the exhibition. My sister is there as we speak—for the third day in a row!"

He smiled almost fondly, which was strange. "She enjoys the paintings, then?"

Kitty snorted dismissively. "Nobody really goes there to look at the paintings, do they? My sister certainly has not. She has gone on a fool's errand to scare off some lecherous tomcat."

"She's not?" Annie said with wide-eyed concern.

Kitty nodded conspiratorially. "She has! I heard her whispering to my aunt about it. Apparently, she overheard Lord Rutherford arrange to meet *another* lady on the couch at the gallery today—"

Annie gasped. "The cheating brute! Sergeant Mulhall was right about him, then?"

"So it would seem. And now Lizzy has it in her head that she must intervene to save the woman from being importuned."

"Is that wise?" the officer interjected with excessive concern. "If my batman has said this chap is a rotten apple, he must have had just cause, in which case, I cannot think it good sense for your sister to seek out his company."

"I agree, it is quite ridiculous," Kitty replied. "As though *she* could prevent a practised seducer from doing anything he likes! But you do not know my sister, sir. She is as obstinate as the day is long. Once she has an idea in her head, she will not be moved."

She could have sworn the officer rolled his eyes as he

muttered, "Sounds familiar," but after that, he seemed to form a new resolution. "It has been delightful, ladies, but if you are sure you are unharmed, I must take my leave of you now." He touched the brim of his hat and began walking away, calling over his shoulder, "I shall tell Mulhall to meet you tomorrow at the British Institution at noon, madam. Good day."

"But I do not want to go there!" Kitty called after him. It fell on deaf ears; he was walking with long strides and evidently out of earshot already. She let out a growl of consternation and repeated to the maid, "I do not want to go to the stupid exhibition!"

"There are worse places to meet than a picture gallery," Annie replied. "*This* place, for one."

Considering the corpses lurking beneath their feet, the stains on her gown, the old man still chasing his sheep in circles in the corner of the field, and the complete want of any romantic assignation, Kitty could not but agree. With jaded sighs and a shake of their heads, the two ladies set off in the direction of home.

CHAPTER TEN

The money-taker at the front desk raised his eyebrows at Elizabeth when she handed over her entrance fee. She tried her best to ignore him—she could not possibly be the only person to have visited so often—but his mockery only exacerbated her vexation to be at the exhibition for a third time in as many days.

She took her aunt's arm and directed her towards the stairs. "I thank you sincerely for coming with me, but I have been thinking—it is probably best if I speak to Miss Darcy alone. It is a delicate subject—I should not like to embarrass her."

"I have been wondering the same myself," Mrs Gardiner replied. "It is a shame, for it would have been nice to talk to her, but I agree—it would be best if I remained discreet."

They reached the landing and with a nod of thanks,

Elizabeth set out through the crowds towards the couch at the end of the upper east room. She did not get far before her steps slowed. She had been focused on helping Miss Darcy evade disaster, but now that she was approaching the interview, the reality of speaking to Mr Darcy's sister loomed large.

They had not been in company since her own precipitous departure from Derbyshire the previous summer, and there had not been enough time for any real affection to be established between them before that. They had met but twice—once when Mr Darcy brought his sister to call at the inn where she and the Gardiners were staying, and again when she and Mrs Gardiner returned the call. At neither meeting had Elizabeth shown herself to particularly great advantage. On the first occasion, she had been too embarrassed, too nervous to give a good account of herself, and on the second, Miss Bingley had sabotaged any chance she might have had of making a good impression by commandeering the conversation to make insinuations about Wickham.

Then Lydia had eloped, and Elizabeth and the Gardiners had been summoned home, requiring them to renege on their acceptance of Miss Darcy's invitation to dine at Pemberley. Since then, Elizabeth's sister had married the man with whom Miss Darcy had once thought herself in love, and Mr Darcy's affections had evaporated. It did not seem likely the young lady would be pleased to see her.

So preoccupied was she with these reflections that she did not notice her proximity to the couch until she was all but tripping over it. It was impossible, therefore, to avoid the notice of the lady seated upon it; too late to hurl herself behind the pillar to hide again; too late to do anything other than smile weakly as Lady Tuppence Swanbrook firmly patted the empty space next to her and waited with an expectant expression for Elizabeth to sit down. Her heart sank, but there was no getting out of it; to walk away would be to give a direct cut every bit as insolent as the one from which Lady Tuppence had been trying to save her.

She lowered herself onto the couch. "Good day."

Lady Tuppence did not answer immediately. Both ladies sat facing forwards, looking into the room in uncomfortable silence. An older gentleman looked briefly in their direction—a fleeting look which, ending as it did with a disappointed pout, most likely signified a search for somewhere to sit down, but which her ladyship took for something more nefarious.

"The staring has not improved much, has it?"

Elizabeth shook her head. "Actually, I do not think he—"

"If only you had kept your appointment with my cousin, their derision would have been done away with. Why did you not?"

Here it was, then. Elizabeth considered claiming to have misremembered the meeting time, but misdirection had got her into this tangle, and she did not think it could be relied upon to get her out of it. The truth was likely the safest response.

"I am sorry if either of you were offended. I ought to have been honest with you on Monday, but I did not wish to seem ungrateful when you were trying to help me. The truth is, I could not face it. I suffered a very great disappointment last year and the thought of meeting someone new, even just to walk about an exhibition with him, was... I could not bring myself to do it."

Lady Tuppence regarded her appraisingly for a moment or two, then inclined her head. "I am sorry to hear that, though it makes it an even greater shame that you did not meet Rutherford. He might have restored your faith in men."

Elizabeth did her best to conceal her surprise at this remark, though it gave her pause. If Lord Rutherford *was* a cad, he had evidently done an excellent job of concealing it from his cousin.

"I do not need my faith restored," she replied. "I was not ill-used. Quite the opposite, in fact. He was a wonderful man. There were just too many obstacles in the end."

"Pfft! Some men are too easily put off."

"Some are, it is true." She considered whether to expound. It was highly unusual to discuss such things with a stranger, but Lady Tuppence seemed interested, and Elizabeth was grateful for the chance to appease her with friendly discourse. And since it was unlikely that they would ever meet, she did not think Jane would mind if she elaborated a little. "My oldest sister had a suitor once, who was persuaded by his friends to throw her over. In their judgment, she did not love him, and her connexions did not compensate for the want of affection."

"Did she love him?"

"Yes, she did, although not as much as she loves her husband." At Lady Tuppence's querying look, Elizabeth added, "Whom she met *after* Mr Bingley abandoned her. His name is Mr Malcolm. His carriage wheel broke near our home one day last summer, and he and his driver came to the house in search of assistance. The rest is self-evident, for they are married now, and living in connubial bliss in Buckinghamshire."

"This Mr Bingley did her a good turn in leaving, then."

"Yes, and he did her an even greater one by coming back. It was above nine months after he left, but he seemed to expect that he could take up where he left off. I could have told him there was no chance of it, but it scared Mr Malcom into proposing for fear that Jane would choose her first love over him."

"Ah, yes! If you cannot tempt a man by conventional means, then giving him competition is always the next best option. But I am curious—what made you say *your* young man was less easily swayed? I hope you will not mind me observing that your heartbreak rather discredits your claim."

Elizabeth smiled wryly. "He put up with quite a lot before conceding defeat. His affections and wishes outlasted my vilification of his character, my rejection of his offer of marriage, a separation of half a year, and for a while, all the objections of his friends and family."

"For a while?"

"Yes...until his aunt heard a rumour that we were romantically attached and took exception to the idea. She came to my home in Hertfordshire and tried to extract a promise from me that I would never accept an offer from her nephew."

"Shocking! *Did* you promise?"

"I did not, but it did not matter in the end. Other events had occurred by then which clearly eroded his esteem. My youngest sister married a man with whom he could never consent to being connected—and justly so. If I had the choice, I would not pick Mr Wickham as a brother either. But all told, it was one complication too many."

"Your suitor left?"

Elizabeth nodded. "And never came back." She had begun the tale assuming she would be able to tell it impartially, a simple relaying of facts. She ended it with a catch in her voice and a horrible heaviness in her heart. She hoped her distress was not obvious, but Lady Tuppence confirmed that it was when she nodded pityingly.

"It goes that way sometimes. I am sorry for you. But perhaps it is better that you did not meet my cousin. He is a gentle soul. He would not have liked it if your heart was not in it."

For the second time, Elizabeth struggled to keep her countenance. *A gentle soul?* That was hardly consistent with Sergeant Mulhall's account of him. "He is a kind man, then, is he?" she asked warily.

That earned her a sharp look. "What a strange question," Lady Tuppence replied. She narrowed her eyes. "Have you heard somebody say otherwise?"

"I...well, I—"

"Oh, stuff and nonsense! You ought not to have paid it the slightest bit of notice. This always happens."

"What does?"

She let out a sharp sigh. "You recall what I told you about his altogether tiresome pursuits?"

"Forgive me, no. I was a little distracted at the time."

Lady Tuppence had been adamant that a complete catastrophe had befallen Elizabeth and had been almost fanatic in her resolve to extract some manner of greeting or acknowledgement from every person who so much as looked their way. Elizabeth had scarcely thought it necessary at the time and was even more convinced of the redundancy of the endeavour now, but either way, it meant she had paid very little attention to anything that was said about Lord Rutherford.

Now that she applied herself to the matter, however, one rather incongruous memory surfaced. "I do seem to recall that you accused him of being somewhat...dull?"

"So, you do remember—good. Yes, he will insist on politicking, and some of his activities have made him unpopular with a certain set of gentlemen—those who favour the sorts of establishments my cousin is engaged in attempting to have proscribed. They are vociferous in their censure. If some of it has reached your ears, it sadly does not surprise me."

Elizabeth nodded. She supposed that, if Lord Rutherford's name was often mentioned within the context of such insalubrious places, it was conceivable that he might have been mistaken as belonging to the wrong side of the debate. "Campaigning for reform is an admirable undertaking. He must be very sensible if he has not allowed the criticism to put him off."

"He is, but you must not take my teasing too seriously. He is not truly dull. I only say that because he is cleverer than I am. And a good deal quieter."

Elizabeth smiled fondly. "I require no convincing that a taciturn nature can be fascinating."

"Oh? Your beau was similarly reserved, was he?"

"Am I so transparent?" she replied, laughing. "But yes, he was. I did not understand that at first, of course, but once I did, I came to like it very well. He had a wonderful way of attending to my conversations that made it seem as though everything I said was the most important thing in the world. Even when what I said was designed to give him pain, which to my shame, it often was."

Lady Tuppence held Elizabeth's gaze for a few seconds before replying. "You are wholly forgiven for disappointing my cousin. It would have been cruel indeed to introduce him to someone so much in love with somebody else."

Elizabeth felt her cheeks redden, both in embarrassment that her affections should be on such naked display, and unease, for she knew very well that Lord Rutherford had remained disappointed for the grand total of about two minutes before his hopes were redirected towards Miss Darcy. "If he is as wonderful as you have made him sound, then I daresay he will not have to wait long before he meets somebody else. Whoever she is will have much to look forward to by your account."

"Whoever she is will be treated like a queen, for Rutherford is the kindest, most generous man I know. If I were of a gentler disposition, I might marry him myself—I know our mothers would be delighted by the alliance—but I am simply not sweet enough for him. Happily, you and I may rest easy, for he has overcome both our rejections. When you did not turn up yesterday, he had the good fortune to meet a different young lady."

Elizabeth managed to affect a reasonably convincing tone of surprise as she asked, "Oh?"

"Yes, and since I know your heart is steadfastly engaged elsewhere, I shall not scruple to tell you that he was exceedingly taken with her. He did not stop singing her praises all evening. That is why I am here actually. He arranged to meet her again today but has been called away on business. He asked me to pass on his regrets. She ought to be here at any moment, and I do not mind admitting that I am all anticipation to meet her."

Elizabeth was now wholly satisfied that Sergeant Mulhall had been talking utter rubbish when he accused Lord Rutherford of roguishness, and that she had wasted her whole morning and two shillings on a needless crusade. Abandoning her plans, she resolved to escape before Miss Darcy arrived. "Then I shall most happily leave you to it. I must find my aunt. Pray, accept my best wishes for your cousin's happiness. Excuse me."

"Wait." Lady Tuppence reached into her reticule and withdrew a beautiful mother-of-pearl case, from which she took a calling card. She held it out to Elizabeth. "I like you. Call on me."

Elizabeth took the card but privately dismissed all possibility of establishing a friendship with a woman whose cousin might one day marry Mr Darcy's sister. Such a close connexion would be too painful to even contemplate.

"And a word of advice, Miss Bennet. Do not waste too much of your life pining. Take it from a woman in her fifth Season—it will achieve nothing but to make a good many things much harder than they need to be."

It was difficult to know how to answer that, and Elizabeth settled for saying thank you, dipping a quick curtsey, and leaving.

"Did you speak to her?" Mrs Gardiner asked when Elizabeth found her.

"No, but I have changed my mind. You were right; this was a mistake. I should never have presumed to interfere." She ushered her aunt towards the exit, praying Miss Darcy would not arrive before they could get out, for there were no pillars that she might lunge behind in this part of the building.

"I cannot say I am sorry to hear that," Mrs Gardiner

said. "I was not completely comfortable with the idea, as you know. But why the haste?"

"Because if I do not have to speak to her about Lord Rutherford, then I would rather not speak to her at all. I am sorry I wasted your morning, but pray, let us get out of this wretched place before she arrives. If I *never* have to come back it will be too soon!"

CHAPTER ELEVEN

"For the love of all that is holy!" Fitzwilliam muttered as he stormed back to the inn where his horse was tethered. It was obvious what had happened: Mulhall had delivered Darcy's message to the wrong Miss Bennet. *"Definitely her'* my eye! Of all the stupid bloody mix ups!"

There was some vague similarity between the sisters, recognisable only once Fitzwilliam had comprehended the mistake, but that would have been immaterial to his batman, since Mulhall had not accompanied him to Rosings the previous Easter and therefore had never set eyes on Miss Elizabeth Bennet.

That it was not her Mulhall had agreed to meet would be a relief to Darcy. Less so to Mulhall, who had been uncommonly vituperative upon hearing that his plans would be waylaid. The young woman, too, had seemed genuinely disappointed by the failed assignation, which was the reason Fitzwilliam had done what he could to rekindle the flirtation. He did not think Darcy would mind; considering the lengths to which he had gone to secure Miss Lydia Bennet's welfare, Fitzwilliam was reasonably confident that his cousin would prefer that *this* sister not be miserable either.

That was not the problem that concerned him. Darcy's sole object in giving the warning about Rutherford had been to keep Miss Bennet safe. It was not unreasonable to hope that warning had served its purpose—that she would know to stay away from the man—but no! Rather, it had persuaded her to thrust herself directly into the blackguard's path in the pursuit of some other woman's safety.

Had it been up to him, Fitzwilliam would have left her to it. Not that he did not care for her wellbeing, but she was a woman grown, and what business she involved herself in was up to her. But he knew Darcy would be out of his head with guilt if he knew the consequences of his interference. There was no time to ride to Darcy House and inform his cousin of what was occurring at the exhibition, for her sister had said Miss Bennet was there now. Fitzwilliam could see no other solution than to ride there himself and at least try to ensure she was safe.

"What an absolute ruddy shambles!"

"Sir?"

Fitzwilliam had reached the inn—out of breath and sweaty—and his complaint put a frightened tremor in the stableboy's voice. He reassured him with a sixpence and mounted his horse, setting out as fast as the busy streets would allow for the British Institution. He was positively roasting in his regimentals by the time he arrived. His hair was plastered to his head with sweat, and he was sure his face must resemble a baboon's arse after his ride in full summer sun. Still, better that Miss Bennet think him unpresentable than Darcy rough him up permanently for leaving her to meet Rutherford alone.

Nodding to the odd familiar face, he wandered around the exhibition for ten minutes without seeing her. About to give it up as a lost cause, he performed one last turn of the upper rooms and chuckled when he noticed the two columns sticking up above the milling crowds at the far end of one of the rooms. One of them, he supposed, had provided Darcy's hiding place when he saw Miss Bennet here on Monday. He walked closer, more and more diverted by the thought of his cousin cowering behind one, for they were not as large as Darcy had made out—and his cousin was not a small man. He must have been barely concealed.

Between the two columns was a couch, the sight of which stirred a memory of Miss Bennet's sister mentioning that this was where Rutherford had arranged to meet his new paramour. And as happenstance would have it, upon the couch sat a lady, who at that very moment looked up and met his eye. Fitzwilliam's dishevelment, which had moments before been nothing more than a nuisance, instantly became a catastrophe. Just his luck that he should look his worst when the most beautiful creature he had ever beheld was before him. Still, his scruffiness notwithstanding, if this was the woman Miss Bennet intended to save, he was more than happy to perform the rescue in her stead. He tried to smooth his damp hair into some semblance of order and tugged his jacket straight as he approached.

She watched him, unabashed, until he was standing directly in front of her. She did not look perturbed by his approach. Indeed, she did not look like the sort of woman who needed rescuing from anybody, but that was his excuse, and he was not about to abandon it. He bowed. She raised an eyebrow. He felt a twinge of excitement at her boldness.

"Madam, I beg you would excuse my forwardness. I recognise we have not been introduced, but I must ask—are you here for Lord Rutherford?"

He did not miss the flicker of surprise in her countenance as she replied, "In a manner of speaking."

"Ah. I feared as much."

"Feared?"

"Yes. May I?" He indicated the empty space next to her, then sat in it.

"You already have," she said with an air of annoyance.

"Pardon me, but it would be better if I said this quietly."

"Said what?"

Fitzwilliam glanced at her. She was even more striking up close, and he found himself unusually stupid. "Might I, um...might I introduce myself first?"

"You may not."

Fitzwilliam's face flamed even hotter, though not with embarrassment. Something else, much pleasanter, was making him hot under the collar. "Very well," he conceded with a small smile. "But I must say my piece all the same, for I could not bear for a lady as fair as you to be ill-used. Lord Rutherford is not to be trusted. I am sorry if this pains you, madam, but so it is. I beg you not to put yourself into his power, for your reputation would be at stake."

Two spots of colour appeared on the woman's cheeks and her lips plumped deliciously as she pursed them in apparent displeasure. "Pray, what has his lordship done to you that you should have such a low opinion of him?"

Fitzwilliam stumbled over his response. He had not considered that she might require him to support his claim. Between his senior rank and Darcy's elevated consequence, they were, neither of them, often required to account for themselves. "I confess—nothing," he replied. "It is a warning my cousin tasked me with passing on."

"Well, you may tell your cousin that *my* cousin is as decent a man as ever lived, and I do not appreciate him attempting to convince me otherwise."

Fitzwilliam recoiled. "Lord Rutherford is your cousin?"

"He is, and I could not be prouder to own it." She was hissing her words in anger now, her lips no longer plumped but snarling—though strangely all the more captivating for it. "You and your ilk ought to be ashamed, going about slandering a good man for no reason but spite."

"It is not for no reason, madam. I have it on excellent

authority that he has persuaded an innocent young girl to meet him here, this very afternoon."

"Persuaded? You make it sound as though he tricked her into it! I assure you, the invitation was sincerely made, and Miss Darcy accepted it freely and gratefully."

Fitzwilliam almost choked. "Miss Darcy? Miss *Georgiana* Darcy?"

"Yes."

"Over my dead body—she is *my* cousin!"

"That is difficult to credit, since your cousin apparently thinks my cousin is a scourge of London!"

"I have more than one cousin, madam."

She lurched to her feet and stood, looking furiously down at him. "Then I hope for Miss Darcy's sake that more of them are like her than the one who thought it politic to spread slanderous gossip about an innocent man all about town! At least *my* cousin is not lost to all sense of civility and honour."

Fitzwilliam stood, too, and found himself toe to toe with her. "Tell Lord Rutherford to leave Miss Darcy alone."

"Do you see him here, sir? Or her? From where I am standing, the only person accosting a woman he does not know in a public place, forcing her to listen to his nonsense, is *you*."

Damn! He stepped backwards to put some space between them. "I beg your pardon, madam, it was not my intention to alarm you."

"You did not alarm me. You disappointed me."

Somehow, that was the worst slight Fitzwilliam had

ever received. She walked away without another word, and he watched her go, aware that his mouth hung agape and unable to do anything about it. When she had disappeared from sight, he shook his head to clear it and made his way out. His priority must be to discover Georgiana's part in this fiasco, for it savoured far too strongly of Ramsgate for his liking. All considerations of Lord Rutherford's infuriatingly alluring cousin would have to wait.

CHAPTER TWELVE

D arcy tried to distract himself by whatever means he could, but nothing worked, not even a visit from his officiously energetic tailor. He stood, trussed and pinned into the canvas pattern of a new jacket, and remained mercilessly uneasy, plagued with visions of what might be happening in Potters Fields. His tailor fussed and flapped and eventually left. His sister went out and came home again. His butler came and went into his study. At least three books were picked up and immediately discarded, unread. Darcy could think only of Elizabeth.

Would she be pleased to see Fitzwilliam, dismayed not to see Mulhall, or furious to discover that *he* had orchestrated it all? The likelihood of her being grateful that he cared enough to involve himself and sending her regards was too trifling to waste a scrap of hope on it—so, of course, that is what he spent the chief of the morning wishing for. The minutes ticked by—each seeming to last an hour—until he thought he would go mad waiting for news.

There had been a time, at the beginning of his acquaintance with Elizabeth, when such incessant introspection and uncertainty had frightened him. Far too many chances had been squandered as a result, as he attempted to repress his feelings so that nobody—least of all himself—could deride him for weakness. He was better used to it now, having spent the best part of two years feeling this way. That made it no less objectionable, and by no means easier to endure; thus when he heard the front door slam and Fitzwilliam's voice echo along the hall, he leapt from his chair as though he had been stung.

His apprehension intensified when he heard his cousin calling for him, repeatedly and angrily, as he made his way through the house, and erupted into blistering alarm when Fitzwilliam burst into the room and demanded, "Is Georgiana here?"

"Yes, she got back not long ago. She has gone upstairs to change. Why, what has happened?"

"I shall tell you what has happened. That cur Rutherford has turned his sights on her!"

Darcy stared at him, no less baffled than appalled by the complete non sequitur. "What?"

"You heard! The scoundrel is planning to seduce your little sister."

"Did Elizabeth tell you this?"

"I did not see her."

"You did not—" Darcy paused to swallow an imprecation. "Please do not tell me something came up at the barracks again."

"Would that it had! Then I might not have spent the morning hanging around the arse end of London, waiting for the wrong bloody sister, when I clearly ought to have been here, watching over yours!"

"The wrong—? For the love of God, would you *please* tell me what is going on?"

Fitzwilliam began pacing up and down, shaking his head as he went. "I went to Potters Fields as you asked and spent most of my morning walking up and down the same four paths, waiting for Miss Bennet to show up. Which she never did."

"Oh." Darcy knew not whether to rejoice that she had decided against Mulhall or despair that he had been denied yet another opportunity to hear news of her.

"Shall I tell you who *did* turn up?" his cousin continued.

"Not Georgiana?"

"Oh, no. That would have made everything far simpler. No, the young lady I picked up off the ground after she was bowled over by a rampaging ewe, was not Miss *Elizabeth* Bennet. I see from your face that you have deduced the rest. Mulhall gave your warning to the wrong Miss Bennet."

Darcy closed his eyes in vexation. "Which one?"

"I have no idea, and what does it matter? That is not the salient point."

"Well, what is?"

"Miss Bennet was not there because, according to her sister, she was at the blasted exhibition, in search of Rutherford."

"*What?*"

"Oh, do not concern yourself, she was not there."

"How do you know?"

"Because I *was* there, and I did not see her."

Fitzwilliam's pacing, coupled with his rambling explanation, was driving Darcy distracted. "Speak plainly, man!"

"I am trying to!" his cousin retorted angrily before standing still and rubbing a hand over his face. "Rutherford has lived up to his reputation by throwing Miss Bennet over in favour of a different young girl."

Darcy went cold. "Georgiana?"

The turn of Fitzwilliam's countenance confirmed it.

"Or at least, so I later found out, although I did not know it at the time. All I knew at that point was that somehow Miss Bennet had wind of an agreement the pair made to meet today at the exhibition. And after receiving your warning via her sister, she decided she must intervene to save Georgiana from Rutherford."

"Bloody hell—I was trying to keep her away from him!"

"Precisely why I rode across town to intervene in her intervention. Only she was not there, and neither was he. Instead, I had the misfortune of becoming acquainted with his cousin."

"And who is he?"

"*She*, and I never discovered her name. She refused to tell me. All I found out from her before she *flounced* off in a snit was that the woman Rutherford was meeting was Georgiana."

"But you said Rutherford was not there."

"He was not."

"Where was he?"

"How the devil should I know?"

They had each grown steadily louder in their responses and this last was all but shouted, bringing Darcy to his senses.

"We are going in circles. We had better speak to the one person who might be able to shed some light on the matter." He rang the bell and, when a footman answered the summons, instructed that Georgiana be asked to join them. He poured his cousin a drink while they waited and thanked him for his efforts that morning.

Fitzwilliam raised his glass in acknowledgement, then took a swig. "I am sorry I did not manage to speak to Miss Bennet. I know you hoped I would."

"It seems we have more immediate concerns," Darcy replied, though it was not true. Whatever was afoot between Georgiana and Rutherford, *she* was here, safe and accounted for. Elizabeth had not been where her sister believed her to be, and to his mind, that was a far greater cause for concern.

His sister arrived not long after, entering the room with altogether too cheerful an air. "You wished to see me? Oh! Good day, Cousin. I did not know you were here, too." Her smile faded when her breezy greeting was met with stony faces.

"Sit down," Darcy told her.

She did, looking nervously between him and Fitzwilliam, though he could perceive no hint of guilt in her expression, and since he well knew what that looked like on her, he did not think he would miss it if she felt any.

He crossed his arms. "Where did you go when you went out earlier?"

The enquiry obviously surprised her, but other than a vague frown, she showed no great alarm at the line of questioning. "To the exhibition on Pall Mall."

"You admit it, then? Without shame?"

"Why should I be ashamed? I did tell you I was going there today."

"But you did not tell us why." This time, Darcy saw her contrition plainly, and it cut him to the quick. It was Ramsgate all over again. "Tell us what you were doing there. And we want the truth, young lady."

She continued to look between them, wincing in distress. "I *will* tell you, and I beg you to believe that I *meant* to tell you, because this makes it seem as though I was deliberately keeping it a secret."

"Keeping what a secret?" Fitzwilliam pressed.

"Upon my word, it is *not* a secret. I was going to tell you last night, but you were both so angry with one another, the opportunity never arose."

"It has arisen now," Darcy said, his struggle to remain

calm giving his voice a hard edge. "What were you doing at the exhibition?"

"I went to meet somebody."

"Lord Rutherford?"

Georgiana's eyes widened. "You knew?"

Darcy looked at Fitzwilliam; he had pinched the bridge of his nose and was silently shaking his head. Darcy shared his consternation. After everything that had happened with Wickham, he had not thought his sister could be so foolish again.

"Please, let me explain," Georgiana said plaintively. "It is not what it sounds like—this is not the same as what happened before, I swear it."

Fitzwilliam made a noise of disbelief. "You have concealed a clandestine liaison from us. It is exactly the same."

"Let her explain," Darcy said darkly. "I would hear what this blackguard is playing at."

"Blackguard? Oh, no, he—"

Her naivety was infuriating, and he snapped "Explain!" more brusquely than he meant to. It made her sullen.

"We met by accident when I was there yesterday. He thought I was someone else, but after we cleared up the confusion, we talked for a while about the paintings. He was knowledgeable and kind, and when he suggested we meet again today to continue our conversation, I agreed. Mrs Annesley was with me. It was all very proper."

Darcy shook his head in disbelief. "There is *nothing* proper about rendezvousing with a man to whom you have not been formally introduced and whom neither of us knows. A man, I might add, of negligible honour and ignoble reputation."

Her face contracted as though he had spoken to her in High Dutch, and she shook her head. "I refuse to believe it."

"Oh? And pray, on how long an acquaintance is your good opinion founded?"

"At least I *have* met him! You just admitted you do not know him at all."

Darcy did not much care for the defiance that was blossoming along with Georgiana's womanhood. "I know *of* him. His reputation precedes him."

"And I have met his cousin," Fitzwilliam piped up. "She is proof enough for me that the whole family is trouble."

"But Lady Tuppence is lovely!" Georgiana cried.

"When did you meet his cousin? You only met *him* yesterday. Is he already introducing his relations? Moves fast, does he not?"

"I met her today, at the exhibition. She came to tell me that Lord Rutherford had been called away on business and wished to postpone our meeting until tomorrow. And he would not have sent her to do that if he was as awful as you say. He would have just left me waiting and wondering."

The prospect that Rutherford's 'business' was somehow connected to Elizabeth's absence from the exhibition troubled Darcy exceedingly. "Well, it will be your turn to leave him waiting tomorrow, for you are not going back to that exhibition."

Georgiana exclaimed theatrically, then launched into a stream of entreaties as she begged him to reconsider, impressing upon him the strength of feeling Rutherford had stirred in her. Then, perhaps recognising that this was not likely to succeed, she tried instead to persuade Fitzwilliam and him that they, too, would like Rutherford, sketching a picture of his character so detailed that Darcy began to doubt they could only have met once.

She did not mention—because she could not know—that Rutherford frequented brothels and gambling dens, that he had a reputation for being a cad, and that he had heartlessly cast off the finest woman of Darcy's acquaintance in order to work on her. To hear her singing the man's praises was sickening.

"If you would come with me," she pleaded, "you would see for yourself! You could—"

"An excellent idea," he interrupted.

"What?" Georgiana and Fitzwilliam both said at once.

"*You* are not going anywhere," Darcy told his sister. "But I shall go, and I shall tell Lord Rutherford to cease trifling with all the people I love!"

CHAPTER THIRTEEN

"Do you see that one—the third along from the corner—with the stormy sky?"

"Yes."

"Good. Now, look closely at the one beneath. The tiny one with the gilt frame twice the size of the canvas."

Kitty peered at the painting in question, but it was too high to see clearly. Sergeant Mulhall produced a pair of opera glasses from somewhere and passed them to her with a small smirk. She looked again and snorted inelegantly with laughter. There, in the corner of the diminutive painting, was an elderly man, in all his glory, bending over to wash his hands in a stream. That took their count of bare bottoms to forty-two.

"I told you there were more to be found," he said. "Painters are nothing but lecherous old men, really. Art is merely their excuse."

They moved along a bit, and Kitty saw Annie step

nearer to the wall behind them and look up at the same painting, her face screwed up tightly as she tried to determine what had diverted them. She wished the maid would comprehend that one did not need to be within touching distance to be an effective chaperon, but she would insist on trailing them about like a nervous shadow.

Sergeant Mulhall showed no sign of being troubled by it. He had excessively happy manners—polite without being at all stuffy. He had apologised profusely for not keeping his engagement the previous day and wholly agreed with Kitty's lamentations about the choice of venue for this consolation tryst. They had agreed to make the most of it, though, and were both finding great pleasure in making sport of that which everybody else was pretending to take so seriously.

"Would you allow me to call on you properly, Miss Bennet?" he said abruptly.

Kitty preened with pleasure. "I would, but I must warn you, my aunt and uncle may not approve. They have rather gone off soldiers since my sister married one they do not like."

"I shall have to work hard to change their opinion then, shan't I?"

She smiled broadly, excessively flattered, though another thought soon obtruded onto her happiness. Where she might ordinarily have applied to Lizzy for help convincing Mr and Mrs Gardiner that not all members of His Majesty's Army were bad news, her sister's opinion of this *particular* officer was such that her assistance was not guaranteed.

This, Kitty had discovered the night before, when just as she was falling asleep, Lizzy had whispered into the dark that she was sorry not to have gone with her to meet Sergeant Mulhall that day, but that she was glad of it now. Pressed to explain why, her sister had relayed a conversation she had had that afternoon with Lady Tuppence Swanbrook, who had given such a solid defence of Lord Rutherford's character that it had cast Sergeant Mulhall's account—and his motive in giving it—into serious question.

'I think he might be a troublemaker,' had been Lizzy's conclusion, and while that would not have been enough to put Kitty off meeting any man—indeed, was more likely to make her want to meet him than not—it did make her curious to know why he had said it in the first place.

"I have a question for you," she said.

"Steady on, I only asked to call on you."

That made her snort again. "I was wondering why you told me Lord Rutherford is a rake."

"I hope this does not mean I have a rival."

"Not at the present moment," she replied with a coy smile. "It is just that my sister has information to the contrary, and she thinks you must be up to no good to be spreading unfounded reports about people."

"Ah, I see. That is unfortunate, but I hope you will acquit me of calumny when I tell you that I was only following orders. And whilst I cannot personally attest to the truth of the report, I can certainly vouch for the man who ordered me to pass it on."

Kitty ceased searching the array of paintings for additional derrieres and turned her complete attention upon Sergeant Mulhall, her curiosity seriously piqued. Not in a thousand years would she have anticipated such a revealing answer. "Pass it on? I thought the matter merely came up in conversation. Do you mean to tell me somebody sent you with the deliberate design to warn me?"

"Not you, madam. Your sister. When you told me your name was Miss Bennet, I assumed I had found my mark. I would apologise for the mistake, but I cannot be sorry for it, for I would not have had the good fortune to make your acquaintance had I spoken to your sister."

Kitty gave only a cursory smile, too interested in the delicious mystery unfolding before her to be distracted by compliments. "You are very kind but pray tell me—who sent you to warn my sister?"

"My commanding officer, Colonel Fitzwilliam."

It was not a name Kitty recognised. To her knowledge —which was not inconsiderable, whatever her father might think—there had been no Fitzwilliam in either of the regiments encamped near Meryton over the last two years, and Lydia had never listed him among Wickham's fellow officers in the north. "I do not know anyone by that name."

"Your sister does. They met in Kent last year."

"Did they now?"

Lizzy truly was a sly one. It was said that some people

kept their cards close to their chests. Lizzy kept hers stuffed tightly down the front of her stays, never to see the light of day. It had always infuriated Kitty and Lydia, for she was their only sister whose secrets they were never able to extract by some method or other. "But how did he know she was meeting Lord Rutherford?"

"It is strongly encouraged for a soldier not to question his orders," Sergeant Mulhall replied with an enigmatic smile, which might have been attractive if he were not being so vexingly evasive.

"He must be watching her. Should I be concerned? Is he dangerous?"

"Not in the least! He is a fine gentleman. The younger son of an earl."

"He must be in love with her, then," Kitty replied glibly, hoping to provoke him into being more forthcoming. "It would explain why he sent you to warn her instead of coming himself. That would have been too obvious."

Sergeant Mulhall chuckled. "No offence to your sister, I am sure she is delightful, but that is not the colonel's style. But I understand they are good friends. Which leads me to hope this might put me back in your sister's good graces."

Kitty opened her mouth to reply but was forestalled when the woman next to her stepped backwards into her and almost tripped over. Murmurs of "I say!" and "Upon my word, have a care!" went up as a tall gentleman stalked past them all, leaving the crush eddying about in disgruntled circles in his wake.

Kitty gasped in recognition. "That is Mr Darcy!"

"Yes, I know," Sergeant Mulhall replied, frowning. "I wonder what has him all riled up."

"Probably nothing. He always looks cross if you ask me. How do you know him?"

"He is Colonel Fitzwilliam's cousin."

"Is he?" She grinned at the coincidence. What a joke to have accused Colonel Fitzwilliam of interfering, when here was his cousin who had a proven history of meddling in other people's relationships—to Jane and Mr Bingley's detriment. But he had also famously scorned Lizzy's beauty; thus Kitty grinned again as she quipped, "Perhaps it is *he* who loves Lizzy!"

Sergeant Mulhall did not answer her. She stopped craning her neck to peer over the crowds and turned to face him.

"What?" he asked, all faux innocence.

"Upon my life, he *does* love her, does he not?"

"I could not possibly say," he averred, though when Kitty stepped nearer to him and fluttered her eyelashes as Lydia had taught her to, he *did* say, without hesitation, "Yes, he does."

Kitty burst out laughing. "Oh Lord! Mr Darcy, who never had a good word to say about my sister, is secretly so in love with her that he slandered her love interest to prevent either of them forming an attachment!"

Sergeant Mulhall laughed ruefully and made a gesture with his hands for her to lower her voice. "I beg you would not repeat that. I shall not be thanked for saying anything."

"Do not worry, Lizzy will not want to hear it anyhow.

She hates him. Besides, she has decided to marry someone else."

"Indeed?"

"Yes. She is tired of being plagued to find a husband and thinks accepting Mr Knowles will stop everybody pestering her about it all the time."

This was something else Lizzy had disclosed in the dark the previous night, directly after she had snuffed out the candles and thrown herself onto the bed in high dudgeon at being made to listen all evening to Mrs Gardiner's 'advice' on suitable matches.

"Who is Mr Knowles?"

"A business acquaintance of my uncle's. He has been sniffing around Lizzy for an age, so he will be delighted when she accepts his invitation."

"Invitation? I thought you were talking about a proposal?"

"Oh, the invitation is to the special event here tomorrow evening, but everybody knows he will propose while they are here. 'Tis a candlelit event with musicians—he is bound to ask."

"It does seem likely." Sergeant Mulhall returned to searching the paintings, but after a short while said, quietly, "A candlelit event with musicians, eh?"

Kitty gave him a sideways glance. "Yes."

"That does sound terrifically romantic."

"I suppose it does."

"I assume your sister will not come alone. I imagine

certain members of her family will want to accompany her on such a prestigious occasion."

Kitty kept her eyes on the portrait of a spectacularly ill-favoured woman in a stupid feathered headdress in front of her and smiled. "I imagine so."

"What a happy coincidence," Sergeant Mulhall said, bending forwards to closely inspect the same picture. "For I have just this very moment decided that I like paintings after all and ought to return tomorrow to inspect them all again by candlelight."

Kitty leant forwards until her nose was as close to the canvas as his. "I imagine I might see you here, then."

He turned his head to cast her a quick and very close-up smile. "I imagine you will."

CHAPTER FOURTEEN

D arcy had worked himself into quite the lather by midday on Thursday. He seemed doomed to be forever tasked with preventing worthless men from hurting innocent women whilst being perpetually denied his own chances of happiness with the fairer sex. He was more than a little fed up with acting the knight gallant and hoped Rutherford would recede without a fuss, for he was in no humour to be gainsaid.

One thing had kept him from despairing as he lay awake for most of the night, railing at the world for dealing his innocent sister another disingenuous suitor: Elizabeth had wanted to save her. So many questions swirled about that revelation as made his head hurt attempting to straighten the matter out, not least whether Fitzwilliam's intelligence was even correct. But assuming it was, assuming Elizabeth had gone to the British Institution to protect Georgiana from Rutherford's advances, the question Darcy would most like answered was—had she done it for him?

"Upon my word, have a care!" somebody grumbled as he forged distractedly past them. He muttered an apology and kept moving, eager to get the business done.

He stopped when the couch came into view. The same couch with its blasted pillars at each end, where he had heard Elizabeth agree to meet the very man who, presumably, was the one presently waiting upon it for Georgiana. Darcy's lip curled. The cur looked as easy as anything, wholly untroubled by the harm he was about to wreak upon a young girl's reputation and thoroughly ignorant of the pain he had already inflicted on her.

There was something familiar in his countenance which confirmed to Darcy that they probably had met at some point, justifying his niggling recognition of the name. With a nod to himself, he approached the couch and stopped a scant few inches away, forcing the reprobate to crane his neck to look up at him.

"Rutherford, I presume?" he said without preamble.

The man did not react as he expected. Instead of appearing troubled or affronted, he broke into a broad smile. "Darcy?"

"Excuse me?"

"As I live and breathe, it is! Fitzwilliam Darcy!" He stood up abruptly, forcing Darcy to take a hasty step backwards to avoid a blow to the chin, and thrust out his hand. "Well I never! Had I known the connexion, I would have announced myself to you sooner."

Darcy did not shake his hand. "Do I know you?"

"I should hope so! To be so thoroughly forgettable would be tragic."

The fleeting feeling of familiarity Darcy had felt moments before suddenly asserted itself with new significance. His pent-up anger was too great to be easily cut through, however, and the result was a petulant sort of defiance. "And yet..."

"A tragedy I must be!" Rutherford conceded with unperturbed amiability. "I suppose it has been a long time, and I daresay the name has thrown you. I was Lloyd-Sanders at school, but my father has since passed away, and I have inherited the title. I used to be fast with your cousin, Barclay, if you recall. How is he these days?"

"He is overseas," Darcy replied tightly, peering at the viscount with escalating disquiet. "But the last we heard he was well, thank you." As he stared, Rutherford's features slotted slowly but seamlessly into older memories of a younger man's face. Lloyd-Sanders. Charles Lloyd-Sanders. It dawned on him in a rush why Georgiana had been so confused to hear him referred to as a blackguard. "You are not a rake!"

He clamped his mouth closed, privately cursing his vulgar outburst, but this man truly was no libertine. He was the one-time favourite of his own eldest cousin— Fitzwilliam's older brother, Barclay. A chap of prodigiously good character and even better connexions if memory served him correctly. Barclay had not mentioned him in many years, but then, Barclay himself had spent most of the last decade plundering foreign lands for art and artefacts to fill his father's newly refurbished and extended castle. Nevertheless, Darcy recalled the esteem in which his cousin had held the then Lloyd-Sanders. It was all but impossible to imagine the man had strayed into depravity in the intervening years.

"Forgive me." He grabbed the hand that Rutherford still held towards him and shook it. He wished he had done so sooner when the return of the usual level of conversation around him brought to his attention how quiet it had grown. He rued making a spectacle of the encounter and affected a deliberately less antagonistic demeanour to allay any brewing speculation. "I meant no offence, but...I came expecting to find a man of considerable disrepute waiting here to meet my sister."

Rutherford quirked his mouth contritely. "Well, I hope I do not need to convince you of my respectability—but it seems I *am* waiting for your sister. I can only apologise for what must appear a disagreeably clandestine arrangement. I did not realise she *was* your sister you see. I assumed the name was a coincidence and she must be from another Darcy family."

"Are there others?"

"Fewer than I thought this morning, obviously! But I could have sworn you were an only child."

"She did not often come to Matlock with me when she was younger," Darcy admitted. "After my mother died, my father preferred her to stay at Pemberley."

"That vindicates me to some extent, though not entirely. Is he in town? I shall speak to him directly—"

Darcy cut him off with a shake of his head. "He is no longer with us. He died above six years ago. Fitzwilliam and I share the guardianship of Georgiana now."

Rutherford winced in chagrin. "My condolences, Darcy. I am sorry to hear that. Of course, I would know this if I had done the decent thing and called on Miss Darcy at home before arranging to meet her here. The truth is, I had not yet worked up the courage to ask her if I might. We only met two days ago."

That brought Darcy's thoughts spinning back round to the other matter that had been troubling him deeply these past few days. "Yes, about that. Georgiana said you met by accident—that you were in fact waiting for somebody else." He dared not elaborate and hoped his anguish did not show as he waited for Rutherford's answer.

"That is correct—and now I begin to better comprehend the extent of your ire when you arrived just now, for that paints an even worse picture of my conduct, does it not? Let me assure you, it was not a romantic assignation. It was a young lady I never met before, whom my cousin asked me to escort about the exhibition. She never showed up in the end. Fortunately for me, your sister did."

His cousin? The lady who had sat on this couch at the start of the week and described Rutherford to Elizabeth as an out-and-out cad had been the man's own relation? Darcy would not have credited it but for Fitzwilliam's account of her. 'Proof enough that the whole family is trouble,' he had said. Indeed, she must have been truly disagreeable, for Fitzwilliam was not usually so easily riled. He pitied Rutherford such disloyal connexions, but he did not mention it. He was not without meddlesome relations of his own, and he knew from experience it was better not to fan the flames of their resentment. He had made the mistake of exacerbating Lady Catherine's grudge against Elizabeth, defending her against the charge of beginning a rumour that he and she would soon be engaged. The result had been her ladyship's disastrous visit to Longbourn and the crushing end to all his desires. He had no wish to bring the same fate down upon anybody else.

"She is beautiful, Darcy. And so wonderfully well informed."

It took Darcy a moment to comprehend that Rutherford was talking about Georgiana, and not Elizabeth. "Thank you. She was rather taken with you, too."

Rutherford smiled bashfully and looked so much like his younger self that Darcy could not fathom how he had not recognised him straight away.

"That is heartening to know. Indeed, it emboldens me to enquire whether you might consent to me calling on her. Officially."

Darcy gave his consent willingly but privately wondered at the turn of events. He had come fully prepared to call Rutherford out, if need be. He would leave with one of the finest men in England as a serious contender for his sister's affections. It was a most fortuitous outcome, and he welcomed it unreservedly—yet he could not help but feel guilty.

Had he not intervened, it would be Elizabeth on whom Rutherford was calling. He would have loved her instantly, for no man in his right mind could not, and then it would not have been long before she became Lady Rutherford. It would have been a wonderful match, and no doubt a wonderful life, and he had denied Elizabeth all chance of it —though, that in itself was not the cause of his regret. In fact, Darcy was profoundly relieved that the meeting had not taken place—he had only to feel ashamed at the extent of his triumph.

Somebody indicated a desire to sit on the couch and they moved away to allow them access.

"You and Miss Darcy must come to dine," Rutherford said as they made their way through the crowd.

"It hardly seems fair that you should host me when I have turned up here ready to lay all manner of charges at your door."

"Nonsense. It was nothing any good brother would not do. We can laugh about it over a good bottle of merlot. What say you? Tomorrow night at eight?"

"Very well if you insist. I am sure Georgiana will be delighted."

"Excellent! And bring Fitzwilliam, too. I have not seen him for years, and if I am to impress two guardians, I had better make a start on both now."

CHAPTER FIFTEEN

E lizabeth was reclining on the chaise longue in the upstairs parlour, reading the last few pages of her book, when Kitty flounced in and planted herself noisily in the nearest chair. She rested the book face down on her chest and waited to hear what her sister wanted. She knew she would want something; a theatrical entrance was always a precursor to a plaintive request. It was a method Lydia had perfected not long after she first learnt to walk, and which Kitty had not long after adopted.

She did not have to wait long, though her sister's appeal, when it came, made little sense.

"I have decided to come with you tonight."

"Pardon?"

"Do not be funny about it. I promise not to get in your way. But I would like to come."

"What are you talking about? Come where?"

"To the candlelit opening."

"*What* candlelit opening?" Elizabeth cried, exasperated. "Pray, start talking sense or leave me to finish my book."

Kitty huffed in apparent affront. "I thought you might take a little persuading, but I did not think you would be as unreasonable as this."

Elizabeth swung her legs off the chaise and sat up. "Kitty, I do not know what you are talking about. I am not going anywhere this evening."

"Yes, you are! You are going to the exhibition with Mr Knowles—you told me so yourself!"

Elizabeth let out an incredulous laugh. "I was being facetious! I never want to step foot in that place again as long as I live, and I certainly do not want to go there with Mr Knowles."

"But Aunt Gardiner is going with you. I heard her telling you what she plans to wear when I joined you both at breakfast."

"Aunt Gardiner is going with our uncle to the theatre this evening."

Kitty blinked at her, observably deflated. "Then...you are not going to the exhibition?"

"No."

"But you must!"

"Why?"

"Because I wish to go, and you were my excuse."

Elizabeth snapped her book shut and set it aside. "You had better tell me what is going on."

Kitty glared at her as though she were personally

responsible for the downfall of all her schemes and said sullenly, "I am meeting somebody there."

"Who?"

"It does not signify."

Elizabeth took up her book once more and reclined without a word on the chaise longue.

"Oh, very well!" Kitty exclaimed. "I am meeting Sergeant Mulhall."

"When was that arranged?" Elizabeth asked in alarm, sitting up straight again. She listened in astonishment as Kitty admitted to secretly sneaking out to meet the officer not once but twice that week. Her sister betrayed not an ounce of contrition, and by the end of her explanation, Elizabeth was struggling to contain her vexation. It was Brighton all over again, distinguishable from Lydia's misadventure with Wickham only by dint of Kitty not yet having packed her bags and run away!

"I ought to have known something was amiss when you said you were taking the air with Annie yesterday. You hate the air!" When Kitty only rolled her eyes, Elizabeth cried, exasperated, "Have you learnt nothing from Lydia? She ruined her life this way—would you do the same?"

"Sergeant Mulhall is nothing like Wickham."

"No? He is an officer who, without any provocation, has told us lies about an innocent man, and has secretly pursued a lady instead of announcing his intentions openly and honestly to her family. He sounds *exactly* the same to me!"

"He was going to call, but this thing at the gallery came about first."

"How very convenient," Elizabeth replied with a shake of her head and an incredulous frown.

"It was very *inconvenient* actually, Lizzy, for I would much rather talk to him here than at the stupid art exhibition where there is only one seat in the entire building. But just at the moment he was asking whether he might call on me, Mr Darcy stormed into the gallery, and we got distracted talking about him instead, because—would you believe—it turns out Mr Darcy was in love with you all along! But, I said that you had always hated him and that you were meeting Mr Knowles at the candlelit event, and Sergeant Mulhall said the candles sounded romantic, and that is when we agreed we would meet there."

Elizabeth held herself very still and tried to extract some sense from Kitty's diatribe, but it was difficult to focus on anything besides the mention of a certain gentleman. "Mr Darcy was there?" she eventually asked, and rather feebly.

"Yes," Kitty replied impatiently. Then she narrowed her eyes. "You have gone very pale. What is it to you that Mr Darcy was there?"

"Nothing." That was accurate—Elizabeth had long ago forfeited the right to claim that Mr Darcy's business was anything to her, but her heart ached with the weight of that truth. "It has just been a long time since we saw him. Do not change the subject. We are talking about Sergeant Mulhall, whom you will not be meeting at the exhibition or anywhere else, for he is clearly trouble, spreading unfounded rumours and encouraging you to defy your family."

"He has not encouraged anything of the sort—he expressed his anticipation to meet you this evening! It is you who is denying him the introduction by refusing to come with me to the exhibition. And as for the *supposedly* unfounded rumours, you will change your mind when I tell you why he told me Lord Rutherford was a cad."

"I doubt it."

Kitty flashed a self-satisfied smirk at her. "He was following orders. He was instructed to pass on that warning by his commanding officer—Colonel Fitzwilliam."

Elizabeth absolutely started. "What?"

"I thought you would find that interesting. But it gets better. It turns out, the warning was not meant for me—it was meant for *you*. And guess who asked Colonel Fitzwilliam to warn 'Miss Bennet' that Lord Rutherford was a cad?"

"Who?" Elizabeth asked, though so breathily that it was more exhalation than question.

"Why, Mr Darcy, of course!"

"That makes no sense, Kitty. Why would he do that?"

"I told you—he is violently in love with you and did not want you to step out with another man."

It was almost amusing how wrong she was. Elizabeth might have laughed if the words she must say next were not so painful to speak. "Mr Darcy does not love me, Kitty."

"He must! Why else would he stick his nose into your business in this officious manner?"

"The answer to that is simple—he would not."

"He *would!* Do not forget, he has done it before. He warned Mr Bingley against marrying Jane, did he not? And you said he did so because he cared about his friend."

"Yes, that is true." Elizabeth wished her sister would stop.

"And he made Wickham marry Lydia to save her reputation. He takes great pleasure in directing other people's romantic affairs. What makes you think he would not do it again?"

"Because he has no reason to this time."

"Yes, he does—you!"

Elizabeth shook her head, willing her sister to desist. "He *does not love me*, Kitty."

"How do you know?"

"Because he never came back!" she said sharply—and instantly regretted it. She had never disclosed to Kitty what had transpired between her and Mr Darcy. Only Jane, Aunt Gardiner, and Charlotte knew, and their combined pity was more than torture enough. "I am sorry. I did not mean to snap. Can we just—"

"Were you expecting him to come back?" Kitty interrupted. Her piercing look from earlier had returned. "Were you *hoping* he would?"

Elizabeth winced, angry with herself for not being able to think of a pert remark to put her sister off. She was usually quicker witted, but her mind was too full of Mr

Darcy and her heart too heavy with sadness to think of anything.

"Lizzy stop being so secretive for once and tell me what is wrong!" her sister said abruptly. "I know you prefer to confide in Jane, but she is not here, so you will have to make do with me. You never know, I might surprise you. I am capable of being sympathetic, you know."

As shocking as this outburst was, Elizabeth could deny none of it. She *had* kept her dealings with Mr Darcy secret from almost everybody, and she *had* assumed Kitty would not be of any comfort to her.

"I prefer to think of myself as private rather than secretive," she said with chagrin. "But very well, I suppose there is no harm in you knowing. It is true that he did love me, once. Indeed, he asked me to marry him, but I was foolish enough to say no, for I did not know him then as I do now. But we had more dealings with each other in Derbyshire than I let on, and I had thought, at one point, that he had... that we might...that—"

"Upon my word, you love him, too."

Elizabeth shrugged; she had no wish to deny it. "But it was not to be. I made too many mistakes—as did Lydia. I dearly hoped he would come back, but I was not surprised when he did not. Marrying so far beneath him to a woman with no money and four sisters would always have presented a difficulty. But add to that having Wickham as a brother and...well, sometimes love is simply not enough."

"Oh Lizzy, you poor thing! I am sorry."

Elizabeth dropped her gaze to her lap, not wishing to

witness her sister's pity. She whipped her head up again when Kitty continued, "I do not *understand* it, for he is so high in the instep 'tis a wonder he can walk straight, but I *am* sorry."

"How comforting," she said drily.

"I would not be so sure he does not still love you, though. After all, he did try to keep you away from Lord Rutherford."

"Please let the matter drop. He does not love me, and my heart will never mend if I am constantly reminded of it."

"No, of course. Do you know what *would* help it to mend?"

"What?"

"Going to the British Institution this evening and meeting Mr Knowles."

Elizabeth threw her hands in the air. Her sister was incorrigible. "Absolutely not! His being there is precisely the reason I will not accompany you. Did you not just hear me say that I am in love with Mr Darcy? What could possibly make you think that I want to encourage a different man?"

"Oh, fie! Then I shall take Annie."

"Halfway across London after dark? I think not. She is only sixteen. I am sorry, Kitty, but your Sergeant Mulhall will have to be disappointed. You are not going and that is final."

"But Lizzy—"

"If you insist on pushing the matter, I shall inform

Uncle Gardiner what you have been up to, and he will forbid you from going anywhere for the next month!"

She had not intended to be unkind but being forced to divulge her deeply held anguish, only for it to be casually overlooked in favour of her sister's schemes made her angry, and the words tumbled out before she could stop them. Kitty turned red and filled her lungs in readiness to vent her outrage, but before the invective could begin, Elizabeth stood up and flounced out of the room with even greater theatre than that with which her sister had flounced in. She forgot her book and was obliged to relinquish all imminent hope of finishing it.

Good, she thought bitterly. She was in no mood for happy endings when her own story remained so dismally incomplete.

CHAPTER SIXTEEN

The carriage rolled along at a snail's pace, stopping every few minutes for the droves of theatre goers and revellers to pass. It was a hot June evening, and the interior of the carriage was sweltering, making their halting progress even more vexing. They had only a mile and a half to travel; it would unquestionably have been quicker to walk, but walking anywhere was not the done thing in fashionable society, and good sense be damned!

They could not have gone on foot regardless, for Georgiana had already spent too much time and emotion in consideration of her chosen gown for the evening. Trailing her hems through London's dirty streets was a proposition not likely to have been met with much enthusiasm.

Darcy smiled to himself at the thought that Elizabeth would have insisted upon it. His smile faded as a familiar fog of melancholy rolled in after it. It was a sadness that followed swiftly on the heels of every fond reverie, a bitter-sweet mix of affection and regret that he was all the better acquainted with on account of how often he thought about Elizabeth. He sighed quietly.

"My hair feels loose. Is it coming out?" his sister asked, anxiously patting her coiffure.

"Of your head?" Fitzwilliam asked.

"Of the pins," Darcy said to his cousin with a warning look. Lord knew Georgiana was nervous enough without his teasing. To his sister, he replied, "It will only come loose if you keep poking it. Leave it alone. I have told you—you look exceedingly well."

"Indeed, you do," Fitzwilliam added more seriously. "Lord Rutherford is a fool if he is not thoroughly enchanted."

Georgiana looked nervously between them both. "Do you truly like him?"

Fitzwilliam shrugged. "Ask us again at the end of the evening."

Seeing his sister's confidence waver, Darcy hastily added, "We would not have agreed to dine with him if we disapproved."

Georgiana smiled sweetly at him, and he hoped he would not regret his words. If his lordship proved to be a rake after all, Fitzwilliam and he would have to extricate her from the situation with as much expedience and as little contention as possible. He thought it more likely Ruther-ford would be the same affable fellow both Fitzwilliam and he recalled, but they were nevertheless both on their guard for any hint of disingenuousness. Their close association with Wickham had taught them both what signs to look for.

Rutherford met them in person at the door, bowing over Georgiana's hand before she had finished taking off her cloak. "Miss Darcy, you look sublime."

Georgiana blushed deeply but looked pleased.

Turning to them, Rutherford held out his hand and shook first with Darcy, then Fitzwilliam, to whom he said, "It has been entirely too long. Darcy tells me Barclay is travelling. I trust he is keeping well?"

"So we are all assuming, for my mother's sake. And you? You look well. I cannot believe Darcy did not recognise you. You have not changed a bit."

"I did recognise him, once the confusion over names was resolved," Darcy pointed out.

"You did, you did!" Rutherford agreed. "But we need not stand about in the cold when we can reminisce more comfortably in the warm with a drink in our hands." He gestured to the nearest door.

"Hear, hear!" Fitzwilliam cried, and since he was closer to it than anyone else, Rutherford indicated that he should go through first, which he did, with alacrity. The viscount took the opportunity to step in behind him to offer Georgiana his arm.

Very sly, Darcy thought as he followed after them all. He frowned when a female voice from within the next room said uncivilly, "Oh, it is you. I was hoping Miss Darcy would be accompanied by one of her less irksome relations."

"Tuppence!" Rutherford said through gritted teeth as he relinquished Georgiana's arm and hastened into the room. "You promised me you would behave."

Georgiana paused to glance anxiously over her shoulder, mouthing, "Lady Tuppence!"

Darcy did not wonder at her bewilderment, for the woman sounded much more in accordance with Fitzwilliam's description than Georgiana's. He gestured for her to keep walking.

"Pray, do not behave on my account," he heard Fitzwilliam say in a tone that seemed entirely too cheerful for the circumstances.

"Have you brought your cousin with you?" the woman asked.

Georgiana had not taken Darcy's advice and remained rooted to the spot, nervously wringing her hands together.

"This is Colonel Fitzwilliam," Rutherford said. "I told you—Miss Darcy *is* his cousin."

"I meant his other cousin," Lady Tuppence replied. "The one with the decided opinions."

Darcy took Georgiana's arm and gently but firmly walked her into the room. If this pantomime was to continue, he would at least see all the players.

"As it happens, he *is* here," Fitzwilliam was saying, "but I ought to explain. You see, we thought—"

"*You?*"

Darcy looked up, surprised to discover the woman

Fitzwilliam was addressing—Lady Tuppence, he presumed —looking directly at him, her expression one of unqualified outrage. She was handsome, fashionably attired, and betrayed all the bearing and assurance of elevated rank. He had the feeling he had seen her before, though he had no idea where, nor why she might be so angry with him.

She raised a finger to point at him with such fervour that Darcy would not have been surprised if she had stalked across the room to poke him in the chest with it had she not been sitting down.

"*You* had the gall to accuse Rutherford of being a scoundrel? Upon my word! If anyone's conduct has been ungentlemanlike, it is yours, sir."

Georgiana let out a small whimper. Darcy squeezed her arm reassuringly, though he was deeply affronted—more so on account of her choice of words, so like Elizabeth's when she rejected his offer of marriage. He had made considerable efforts to redress the defects in his character since then and did not like being accused of failing. He opened his mouth to reply but was anticipated by Rutherford, who had turned puce with anger.

"Good God, Tuppence, what are you about? This is Mr Darcy—Miss Darcy's *brother*! He is a consummate gentleman!" To Darcy, he said, "I can only apologise, Darcy. This is my cousin, Lady Tuppence Swanbrook, and I have no idea what has got into her."

"Do not be in too much haste to apologise, Cousin," she interposed. "You might be less eager to humble yourself when you hear *this* is the man who has been putting about the rumour that you are a rake, not to be trusted with ladies' reputations."

Fitzwilliam cleared his throat. "Nobody was 'putting about a rumour', madam. As I was trying to explain..."

Darcy stopped listening to him. The vague sense that he recognised Lady Tuppence had grown while she was speaking. It was her voice that brought the recollection flooding back to him with a jolt. "I did not call Rutherford a rake, madam. You did."

Fitzwilliam stopped talking and frowned at him in puzzlement.

"I beg your pardon?" Lady Tuppence demanded with great indignation.

Georgiana had tugged her arm away and was staring at Darcy aghast, but that only made him more determined to prove his innocence.

"I heard you with my own ears. At the beginning of the week, at the exhibition, you told a young lady that Rutherford 'spends more time than is good for him in gambling dens and gin houses—*and worse*'."

"Oh, *very* gentlemanly, Mr Darcy, eavesdropping on ladies' conversations! But I said nothing that was not true. Rutherford...*politicks*." Her pause and the gesture she made with her hands as she searched for the word indicated her distaste for the activity.

"A group of us in Whitehall are working to see such dens of iniquity shut down," Rutherford explained.

Lady Tuppence tilted her head accusingly at Darcy. "There is a certain ilk of men who find this ambition particularly distressing. Are we to assume you are one of them?"

"I shall not dignify that with an answer, madam. I would have thought it was obvious that I was concerned what sort of man you were encouraging the young lady to meet. It was not clear from what you said to her that policymaking was the reason that your cousin frequents illicit establishments. Indeed, quite the opposite—you specifically called him out as a cad."

Lady Tuppence gave a loud, mirthless laugh. "He is not *a* cad—he is *The* Cad! That has been his nickname forever."

Rutherford grinned awkwardly. "My initials. I was christened Charles Andrew David. Though, I was not actually known as The Cad until I was at school. In fact, I believe it was your cousin who first coined that name."

"Barclay?" Darcy looked at Fitzwilliam and groaned inwardly to see him grimacing with contrition.

"Gads—do you know, Darcy, now that Rutherford mentions it, that might be where I heard it said that he was a bit of a cad. Makes sense now."

Darcy stared at his cousin in disbelief. This entire week of mayhem and misdirection, all his failed interventions and sleepless nights had come about on the back of that one, misremembered appellation! He was not much less vexed with Lady Tuppence, whose careless words and strange behaviour that day had further confused matters. Thanks to both, here he now stood, in the home of the man he had unjustly accused, who might very well one day be his brother, looking an utter fool. Darcy abhorred being made to look ridiculous.

"I beg you would forgive me, Rutherford," he said tightly. "The misunderstanding is deeply regrettable. It was only the insistence with which her ladyship was pressing her companion to agree to a meeting she was clearly averse to that gave me such cause for concern."

This did not provide Darcy with the exoneration he had anticipated. Lady Tuppence's mouth set into a hard line, and she raised a solitary, reproachful eyebrow and stared at him for longer than was comfortable before replying in a disdainful voice.

"I would not have been in such a rage to persuade Miss Bennet to meet Rutherford, had she not so desperately needed the panacea of his consequence to repair her damaged reputation—damage *you* caused, when you gave her the cut direct in front of the entire assemblage of the British Institution."

"I am afraid I do not take your meaning, madam. I have not, and never would, give any lady, least of all that one, the cut."

"*Au contraire*, Mr Darcy. I could call fifty witnesses to attest to the fact that last Monday morning, you walked into the upper east exhibition room, halted in your tracks upon seeing Miss Bennet, looked her directly in the eye for long enough that nobody could mistake it for a fleeting glance, then turned your nose up and left again. The whole place was scandalised."

"I did no such thing," Darcy said with a strength of

conviction that he was far from feeling. Indeed, as the seconds ticked by, an appalling sense of being very, very wrong began to creep over him.

"Oh my! I think you might have done," Georgiana whispered in a distressed tone. "We did leave very suddenly because you had seen her if you recall."

He was not likely to forget it. He had almost cried out when he spotted Elizabeth mere feet in front of him—had only been saved from doing so because the sight of her had quite literally taken his breath away. He knew he had stared, too, because he had been unable to tear his eyes away from her while his head and his heart battled over whether or not he ought to speak to her. In the end, his head had won, and he had turned on his heel, grabbed Georgiana's arm, and all but dragged her out of the exhibition before Elizabeth could notice either of them.

They had made it as far as the pavement before his heart overruled his head and persuaded him that such an opportunity ought not to be thrown away. He had left his sister waiting in the carriage and gone back in to search for Elizabeth. Except, by the time he returned, she had attached herself to someone new—Lady Tuppence, he now understood—and he had spent the next ten minutes skulking behind pillars and eavesdropping on conversations, before ultimately leaving without ever saying a word.

The possibility that he had done far worse than failing to talk to her—that he had inadvertently given her the worst conceivable form of public insult, that she must have seen it and thought it was intentional, and that she was suffering society's scorn as a result of it—was so distressing, it took him a moment to comprehend that Lady Tuppence had asked him a question.

"Pardon?"

"Miss Bennet—do you mean to tell me that you *know* her?"

"I do, yes." Darcy's ears were ringing.

"My cousin is as generous as the most generous of his sex, madam," Fitzwilliam said, "but he is nevertheless not generally given to trying to resolve the romantic difficulties of young ladies he does not know. All three of us are acquainted with Miss Bennet, and happily so."

Rutherford gave a little grunt of surprise. "Then—and I hope you will forgive me for asking—why did none of you approach her directly with your concerns?"

Darcy could scarcely order his thoughts, which must be why he could not think of a single rational answer to this. "I had reason to believe she would not wish to speak to me," he mumbled at length.

"Well, I can see why!" Lady Tuppence said, laughing genuinely now. "A shocking way to behave, even if it was by accident. The irony being, of course, that despite your best efforts to save Miss Bennet from Rutherford's wicked ways, it would seem that *you* are the only cad among us, Mr Darcy."

She evidently thought this was vastly amusing, and Darcy supposed he ought to be grateful when everybody else joined in her mirth, for it broke the tension and allowed them to laugh their way out of the inauspicious beginning. He did his best to share in their amusement, and when the chance came to change the subject, he seized it with both hands. He gave Georgiana frequent encouraging smiles, nodded 'yes' to Fitzwilliam's every silently sought assurance that he was well, and even managed to make Lady Tuppence laugh once or twice.

Privately, Darcy was despairing. He had not liked to think that he would never see Elizabeth again, but he could have borne it much better knowing that, wherever she was in the world, she did not think ill of him. He smiled at something Rutherford said and felt the expression stagnate on his face as he considered that now, Elizabeth would despise him forever.

CHAPTER SEVENTEEN

Colonel Fitzwilliam put a finger to his lips to silence the waiting footman, then leant closer to the drawing room door and listened carefully. He felt a frisson of pleasure to hear Lady Tuppence's dulcet tones within. He might have baulked upon first seeing her —their previous meeting having gone so badly—but her first words were so cutting, and her bright eyes so piercing, she had slashed through all his lingering resentment in an instant. With all impediments out of the way, he had been quick to conclude that she was a truly magnificent creature —fierce, loyal, indecently attractive. She was also rich, which gave him leave to advance his admiration from the hypothetical to the earnest.

She had been vastly entertaining throughout dinner, perhaps even intimidating Georgiana a little, for his young cousin had not said a great deal. It was not that Lady Tuppence was in any way unkind; Fitzwilliam merely fancied that she had little interest in mollycoddling fainter hearts than her own. That she had so easily forgiven Darcy and him their blunder was testament to her goodness—as was her attempt to assist Miss Bennet. Fitzwilliam was particularly grateful that she had not sustained her criticism on that subject for long, for he did not think Darcy would have held up to it well.

He was not fooled for a moment by his cousin's feigned sanguinity. The colour had drained from Darcy's face when he realised what he had done, and it had not returned since. Fitzwilliam felt for him—it was an exceedingly unfortunate mishap—though it was all somewhat moot at this point in proceedings. Darcy had, himself, forsworn any possibility of re-establishing the acquaintance before this disaster happened—but even had he not, there would be no chance of doing so now. For, assuming the intelligence Fitzwilliam had received earlier that day from Mulhall was correct, Miss Bennet's happiness and protection were about to become somebody else's concern, and whatever Darcy may or may not have done to offend her would soon be irrelevant.

Fitzwilliam was a man trained in battle, however, and he knew that a war was not won by giving up one's own position simply because one's ally had been shot down. He tossed the footman a sixpence for his patience and let himself into the drawing room.

"Ladies! I hope I am not interrupting?"

"You hope no such thing," Lady Tuppence replied with a small but thrilling smirk.

146

"True." He joined them where they were sitting on two long couches, arranged perpendicularly to the fireplace, though the fire was mercifully unlit. He sat next to his cousin, facing Lady Tuppence, whose gaze he held as he added, "Quite deliberate."

"Where are the others?" Georgiana enquired.

"Deep in conversation about soil drainage or something equally tedious. I left them to their brandy and came in search of livelier company."

Georgiana looked relieved, which was intriguing.

"Why?" he asked. "Were you talking about something you would not like them to hear?"

"Yes," Lady Tuppence answered. "We were talking about Mr Darcy."

"Were you indeed?"

Georgiana blushed and began to stammer an explanation, but her ladyship interrupted to say, more intelligibly, "I asked Miss Darcy why her brother said earlier that he did not think Miss Bennet would like to speak to him. She was just telling me that he and Miss Bennet were romantically attached at one point."

Fitzwilliam looked sharply at Georgiana. How was it that she could be too timid to open her mouth for most of dinner but have brio enough to blab about her brother's love interests at the slightest provocation? Would the girl never learn? Elopements, illicit rendezvous, inappropriate gossip—the accepted etiquette of affairs of the heart seemed to have entirely passed her by.

"About a year ago, yes," he replied carefully. "It all went off."

"I see," Lady Tuppence said pensively. "In that case, I can see why he thought she would not like to speak to him. No woman who has had her heart broken wishes to have salt rubbed in the wound. It is a little rich, though, that he should claim such great concern for which men she chooses to associate with when it was he who threw her over."

Fitzwilliam bristled at that but thought it best to say as little as possible on the matter. Darcy would not thank him for prolonging the debate. "That is not an entirely accurate account of what happened, madam, but—"

"No indeed! My brother did not break Miss Bennet's heart—she broke his!"

"Georgiana, this is neither the time nor the place," Fitzwilliam said in a low voice.

"But Lady Tuppence already thinks he is a cad who goes about giving ladies the cut direct. We cannot allow her to think he breaks people's hearts, too." Turning to her ladyship, she pleaded, "I beg you would not think ill of him. He is so good. He did not throw Miss Bennet over. He was in love with her."

Fitzwilliam groaned and rolled his eyes. Darcy would roast them both alive when he heard about this.

"I suppose she might have been talking about a different man, although it does not seem likely, given the timings," Lady Tuppence acknowledged. "Colonel, do you know whether your mother has ever visited Miss Bennet's home?"

"Not to the best of my knowledge. Why do you ask?"

"Apparently the aunt of Miss Bennet's love interest travelled all the way to Hertfordshire to forbid her from ever marrying him."

Fitzwilliam sat bolt upright. Propriety be damned—if this was true, it mattered far more than Darcy's pride. "My mother did not go—but my aunt did. Lady Catherine de Bourgh is aunt to both of us. *She* went to Miss Bennet last autumn but was told unequivocally that there was no affection to be opposed, and no alliance would ever be agreed to."

"Well for heaven's sake!" Lady Tuppence cried. "Who listens to their aunt for advice on such matters?"

"*Everyone* listens to Lady Catherine," Georgiana said solemnly.

"Well, your brother should not have, because she has lied to him. Miss Bennet refused to promise that she would never accept an offer from Mr Darcy and was devastated when he did not come back." She reached to pat Georgiana's knee. "We are all delighted that you and Rutherford have hit it off, my dear, and I daresay it has all worked out for the best—but the only reason you had occasion to meet that day is because Miss Bennet was too heartbroken to submit herself to an hour in another man's company and did not keep the appointment."

"But this is wonderful!" Georgiana exclaimed. "Brother will be in raptures."

"It is not quite as wonderful as you might think," Fitzwilliam said. "Miss Bennet has gone to the British Institution this evening as the particular companion of a different gentleman. I understand it is generally expected that he will propose during the course of the evening—and that she will accept."

Georgiana gasped. "Oh no!"

"This does not seem consistent with what Miss Bennet has said to me about her feelings," Lady Tuppence said with a frown. "How have you come by this information?"

"Via my batman, who has struck up an acquaintance with Miss Catherine Bennet—Miss Elizabeth Bennet's sister."

"Is he reliable?"

Fitzwilliam shrugged. "He gives a fine field report. This seems no different."

Her ladyship gave a short, impatient-sounding sigh. "Then this is my fault. I advised her to waste no more time pining. I confess, I did not expect her to run out and offer herself to the next man she met in the street, but I did impress upon her the dangers of waiting too long on a hopeless situation."

Fitzwilliam groaned again. Having been informed that Miss Bennet was now aware of his interference and knowing that Mulhall would see her this evening, Fitzwilliam had sent his apologies, along with his best wishes for her imminent engagement. He had been trying to eliminate any ill will, but in this new context, he comprehended that it would look more like confirmation that she should settle for this other fellow.

"And all this time Darcy has been convinced it was *her* affections that had faded!" He ran a hand over his face. "What a pair! And what a time to discover the mistake!"

"There might still be time to prevent it. We must tell him directly," Georgiana said urgently.

"Tell whom what directly?"

They all whipped around at Rutherford's voice. He and Darcy strolled into the room, his lordship going to the sideboard to begin pouring drinks and Darcy coming to stand next to the couches. The awkward pause of three people unwilling to admit what they had been discussing stretched between them. Their reluctance was understandable; nobody would wish to receive such news in such a setting—least of all Darcy, the most private man Fitzwilliam had ever known—but there was no way of making it more palatable. If there was any hope of the situation being salvaged, then the matter must be explained, and quickly.

He opened his mouth to ask Rutherford if there was somewhere private he might speak to his cousin, when Georgiana took it upon herself to summarise the matter for everyone.

"Brother, Miss Bennet is still in love with you, but unless you can stop her, she is going to accept an offer from somebody else this very evening because she thinks *you* do not love *her*."

Darcy remained very still for what felt like a very long

time—long enough that Fitzwilliam genuinely began to worry that he was suffering an apoplexy—before eventually saying, "What?"

The bubble of silence popped as Fitzwilliam, Lady Tuppence, and Georgiana all spoke over each other in their attempt to explain the tangle of misunderstandings that had just been uncovered. Darcy bore the indignity of having his private business aired in front of two relative strangers and his younger sister with a stillness that was decidedly unnerving. He looked alternately stricken, appalled, livid, and frankly plain ill as he listened, but he said not a word and scarcely moved a muscle. Not while Lady Catherine's lies were laid bare, not while he learnt about the months-long misapprehension between him and Miss Bennet, not while Lady Tuppence relayed all that had been said to her on the subject or while Fitzwilliam repeated Mulhall's report. Not even when all the explaining was done and everybody fell back into silence, watching him in anticipation of what he would do.

"Did I hear correctly—that this fellow's name is Knowles?" Rutherford said into the quiet.

Fitzwilliam confirmed that it was.

"Is that the Knowles of Knowles and Farnham, the brokers?"

"I do not know. Why?"

"Because if it is, then he really *is* a cad. One of the foremost objectors to my work in government, chiefly due to his staunch patronage of a large number of the establishments I am trying to have closed." He lifted his drink to his lips, looking at Darcy over the rim. "You cannot possibly allow Miss Bennet to marry *him*."

That got Darcy moving. Though he said very few more words other than to make his excuses, he was gone within the minute. After privately wishing him luck and seeing him off, Fitzwilliam sat back down by the fire, this time on the other couch, next to Lady Tuppence.

"Georgiana is right. Darcy is usually far better behaved —this is quite out of character. I hope you will not hold it against him."

"Not at all," Rutherford replied. "It sounds as though he has had a jolly disagreeable time of it. I only hope he manages to speak to Miss Bennet before it is too late."

Lady Tuppence gave a little grunt of disdain. "*I* hope he manages to speak to her without accidentally defiling her reputation, or breaking her heart, or just" —she gestured at the door— "*leaving* halfway through. Upon my word, I have never known anyone so prone to continually give offence wherever he goes."

Fitzwilliam raised his glass to her. "Fortunately, what Darcy lacks in manners, he more than makes up for in his relations."

CHAPTER EIGHTEEN

Elizabeth did not realise she was nodding off until someone cleared their throat from the parlour door. She sat up straighter in her chair, grabbing for her book as it slid off her lap. To her surprise, it was the cook who had woken her. "Mrs Thorne! Is anything the matter?"

The older lady lowered herself into an arthritic curtsey. "Pardon me, Miss Bennet, I was hoping you might know where Annie's got to?"

"I am afraid not, why—has she gone missing?"

"She has, ma'am. I wondered whether you or Miss Catherine had tasked her with any errands that would explain her absence," Mrs Thorne replied.

Elizabeth glanced around the room. Then she looked at the clock. Her aunt and uncle had departed for the theatre well over an hour ago. When they left, Kitty had been at the little table in the corner playing Patience. Elizabeth had not heard her leave. A sense of foreboding washed over her. "I shall speak to my sister. She may know something." Mrs Thorne thanked her and shuffled away.

Elizabeth took a deep breath, which did little to alleviate her misgivings, then took up a candle and made her way into the next room. For if she wished to speak to Kitty, she would first have to find her. The morning room was empty, as was their shared bedchamber, as was every other room in the house. Increasingly convinced she knew where both girls were, Elizabeth returned to her bedchamber and opened the closet. It was no great surprise to discover her sister's favourite gown missing. She growled in frustration. Kitty had gone to the exhibition.

She deliberated for a short while about whether it would be better to send for her uncle or go herself to intercept the wayward pair. Doing nothing and merely waiting for her sister to return was not an option. Quite apart from the dangers of two young girls gallivanting about London unaccompanied after dark, Elizabeth had enough experience of sisters running off in the night into the waiting arms of officers that she did not have much faith Kitty would come home at all unless she were fetched there.

"Oh, for goodness sake!"

She snatched her own best gown out of the closet and, as best as she could without either her sister or the maid's help, made herself presentable for a candlelit evening at the British Institution. When she was ready, she ran below stairs to the kitchen where she explained to the rather startled cook that Annie had gone with Kitty, and appealed to her uncle's man, Yorke, to accompany her to Pall Mall.

"My uncle has the carriage," she said to him over her shoulder as he followed her back upstairs.

"I shall hail a hackney coach, miss. If you would wait here?"

"Yes, of course. Thank you."

Thus, Elizabeth found herself dressed in all her finery, pacing impatiently up and down the entrance hall of her uncle's house, fuming with her sister, and railing at the nameless stranger who had given her the cut direct which began this whole vexatious chain of events, for without that, Kitty would never have even met Sergeant Mulhall.

She could not help but wish Mr Darcy were there, for he had saved one of her sisters and would no doubt make short work of rescuing a second. But that thought drew a sad laugh from her—the news that *another* of her relations had disgraced herself could only make Mr Darcy triumph anew at his lucky escape. Besides, as she had told Kitty, he had absolutely no reason to involve himself in her affairs, for he did not love her.

A door opened, and she turned around, ready to leave, but froze on the spot upon coming face-to-face with Annie. Annie, who had come not through the front door, but from Mr Gardiner's study, the door to which was permanently locked whenever he was not within, and the key kept on his person at all times. Elizabeth had not even tried the handle in her search of the house, so certain had she been that it would be empty.

"Is my sister in there?"

Annie nodded, wide eyed, and Elizabeth stormed past her, calling for Kitty. "How did you get in here? I have been looking for you *everywhere!*"

She came up short upon entering the room. Someone— presumably Annie—had filled it with candles. There must have been two dozen at least. Elizabeth dared not think what her aunt would have to say about that. Kitty, in her best gown and with her hair beautifully arranged, was standing in front of the wall on which were hung several of Mr Gardiner's favourite paintings. She was hugging herself and crying.

"Oh, Kitty," Elizabeth said gently. "What are you doing?"

"Pining for what I have missed." This was followed by a loud sniff. "It was going to be so romantic."

Since she was behind her sister and therefore out of sight, Elizabeth gave in to the temptation to roll her eyes. It was all excessively theatrical, even for Kitty. Still, she did not like that her sister was distressed. She stepped closer and put an arm around her. "I am sorry you could not go."

Kitty only shrugged at first—until she looked at Elizabeth properly. "Why are you wearing that?"

"I thought you had gone to the exhibition. I was on my way to find you."

Her sister gave a wordless cry and wrenched herself

free of Elizabeth's grip. "You *would* think that! What must I do to prove to you all that I am not Lydia?" She crossed her arms and added, sullenly, "I am not *you* either!"

"What does that mean?" Elizabeth asked, wounded.

"It means, I do not want to hide away, wallowing in misery for the rest of my life any more than I want to run off and live in ruin and disgrace."

"I am not wallowing in misery!"

"No? What would you call it? You are convinced that Mr Darcy does not love you, but you will not take the chance to be happy with anyone else. You would rather stay at home and fall asleep in your chair like an old woman. Well, I do not want to do that! I wanted to see Sergeant Mulhall."

After a moment to absorb her sister's barbs, Elizabeth said with studied composure, "I am sure that in time you will—"

"He liked me, Lizzy! Nobody ever likes me," Kitty interrupted. "They always like Jane because she is handsome, or you because you are witty. Or they like Lydia's boldness or Mary's godliness. Nobody ever notices me. Sergeant Mulhall was the first. And I really liked him. Just because you are determined to refuse every bit of interest any man shows in you, I do not see why both of us should be alone and unhappy."

She stopped talking, and the room fell into silence. Elizabeth heard the front door open and the muffled sound of Yorke and then Annie's voices. Kitty remained where she was, staring dejectedly at the floor, looking every bit the candlelit, romantic heroine she had evidently been aiming for. She looked very pretty, in fact. And she was right; Elizabeth was wallowing. Jane and Mrs Gardiner had been telling her so for months. As had her mother, in her own way, when she sent her to London to find a husband. Even Lady Tuppence had told her to waste no more time on a hopeless situation. It was a difficult truth to accept, but she ought not to blame Kitty for speaking it aloud.

Elizabeth came to a decision. "You are right. You should not give up this chance. And I should like to make the acquaintance of this Sergeant of yours. Let us go to the exhibition."

Kitty looked up so quickly it was a wonder she did not hurt her neck. "Do you mean it?"

"I do. It is late, but I do not think it is too late. We are both dressed for it. Yorke has a hackney coach waiting. What is to stop us?"

There was nothing, other than the tight knot in Elizabeth's stomach which she was doing her best to ignore, and in short order, they were in the coach on their way across town.

Elizabeth was mesmerised by the transformation at the gallery. A forest of candelabras had been brought in and cleverly arranged to complement the paintings in different and fascinating contrast to daylight. The architecture of the building itself was emphasised to majestic effect. Musicians played in one of the upstairs rooms, and people had taken to whispering, giving the whole place an ethereal, almost hallowed feel. She was enthralled.

She came to her senses when Yorke excused himself to wait in the servants' area. She thanked him and went with Kitty to join the people meandering about the exhibition. There were fewer than there had been on every other visit, no doubt due to the lateness of the hour, and she did not have to fight as hard or wait as long to view each painting.

"How *did* you get into Uncle's study?" she asked as she looked.

Kitty was bouncing on her tiptoes, impatiently searching the room, and answered distractedly. "I picked the lock."

"Kitty!" It was a good thing for her sister that Elizabeth had not asked the question before now, for if she had received that answer when they were still at home, she most certainly would not have rewarded the behaviour with an excursion. "How do you know how to pick a lock?"

"Wickham taught me."

She wished she had not asked, and when a handsome man in regimentals approached them in the next moment, beaming from ear to ear, she had to forcibly remind herself that not all officers were as disreputable as her brother. He had not said more than a few words, however, before the distinction became self-evident. Sergeant Mulhall was well-spoken and civil, with none of the self-important charm she had come to expect from Lydia's husband.

"Miss Bennet," he said, bowing to Kitty. "I am excessively pleased to see you. I began to think you would not come."

"As did I!" Kitty replied. "But here we are—disaster averted. My aunt and uncle were engaged for the theatre this evening, it turns out, but this is my sister, Lizzy. She is the eldest of the two of us, which gives you leave to call me Kitty this evening. Lizzy, this is Sergeant Mulhall."

Something about the exchange struck Elizabeth, and it took a moment for her to realise that it was the want of Kitty's usual giggling flirtation. Her sister spoke to this man as though they had known each other for years, all ease and friendliness. It reminded her of how she and Mr Darcy had conversed, even when they were disagreeing. There had been no undue deference or officious attention from her, no pompous flattery from him. Mr Darcy did not flatter by compliment; he flattered by acknowledging her equal mind and speaking to her accordingly. The memory made her miserable for herself but delighted for her sister.

"Good evening, Sergeant. I am pleased to make your acquaintance."

"That is a good start," he replied. "But I assure you, the pleasure is all mine. Colonel Fitzwilliam has said enough in your praise that I could not have been happy to make the acquaintance of anyone less lovely. He sends his regards, by the way."

"Does he?" Elizabeth said, striving to sound easy. "He has not sent any more messages of whose company I ought to avoid, then?" She tried to make it sound teasing, but her smile felt fixed, and she was sure the heat in her face must expose her as having meant more than she had said. What she really wanted to ask was whether the colonel's warning about Lord Rutherford had truly originated with Mr Darcy, but she had not the courage to enquire, certain as she was that she would not like the answer.

Sergeant Mulhall cleared his throat. "No, madam, but he did ask me to pass on his apologies. He regrets his presumption and wishes you every happiness with Mr Knowles."

"Mr Knowles?" Elizabeth repeated stupidly.

"I told Sergeant Mulhall you were coming here with him this evening," Kitty explained. With a shrug, she added, "I thought you were."

"I see." Here was the answer to the question she dared not ask, then. So far from confirming his cousin's interest in her romantic affairs, Colonel Fitzwilliam had instead sent Elizabeth the clear message that she ought to cease wallowing and marry someone else. *Et tu, Colonel?* she thought wryly.

"Thank you, sir," she replied. "Please tell him that his regards are returned. But you are not here to talk to me. Pray, both of you, go! Enjoy your evening." She gestured to the wider gallery, encouraging them to move away together. "I shall be over here, admiring this painting of a…" She cast a glance at the nearest easel. "Dead fish."

Sergeant Mulhall looked unsure, but Kitty wasted not a moment in snatching up his arm and leading him away. Elizabeth watched them go, fighting prodigiously hard against a swell of jealousy at the way they bent their heads together to whisper to each other.

"Miss Bennet!"

She froze, the knot in her stomach squeezing tighter, for she knew that voice. Never mind that she had been steeling herself for this moment, she still felt unprepared.

Slowly, she turned around and curtseyed.

"Mr Knowles."

CHAPTER NINETEEN

Her uncle's acquaintance seemed displeased to see her—alarmed, almost. "I thought you were not coming this evening."

Before Elizabeth could reply, a woman in gaudy attire and with half an ostrich in her hair appeared at his side, laughing too loudly for the hushed event. She draped most of her upper body over Mr Knowles's arm. "There you are, Dumpy. I thought you had abandoned me." She cast a disparaging look at Elizabeth. "Who is this?"

Elizabeth was not particularly worldly, but even she could guess who—and what—Mr Knowles's companion must be. She supposed she ought to be shocked, perhaps disgusted, certainly wildly offended, yet all she could think as she looked between them was—*Dumpy?* It was a struggle to keep her countenance.

Mr Knowles, who had gone as red as the woman's rouged lips, tried unsuccessfully to prise her off his arm.

"Your uncle assured me you were not coming," he said to Elizabeth. "I did not want to miss the occasion, and Miss Delaney expressed a wish to see the paintings." Every time he pulled one of 'Miss Delaney's' hands away, she replaced it somewhere else, putting him into an ever-greater fluster. "I had already purchased two tickets in advance. It seemed a shame not to use them."

"Quite right, sir," Elizabeth replied. "Why waste a good ticket?"

"Indeed! You are very generous. Dare I hope this means—"

"It means—I comprehend that your affections have found a new home, and you no longer wish to call on me. I assure you, there are no hard feelings. My uncle will *perfectly* understand. Good evening." She inclined her head by the smallest degree and hastened away, smiling to herself to hear him bark at Miss Delaney to let go of him.

It came to something when the discovery that one had been thrown over for a woman of the night was a relief, but this truly was the best thing to have happened to Elizabeth in a long while. Kitty's admonishment, that she was 'determined to refuse every bit of interest any man showed in her,' had not been entirely accurate. Rather, her struggle to repress her true feelings had led to her *not* refusing Mr Knowles's interest.

The truth was that despite all her efforts and everybody else's firm encouragement to be practical, she had not yet learnt to stop loving Mr Darcy. Her endeavours to avoid meeting Lord Rutherford had been powerful proof of that.

She fancied she would be happier if she simply allowed herself to feel it and ceased torturing herself with the notion of giving her heart to anyone else. Her family would be disappointed, maybe even angry, but there was nothing for it. When she resolved to come this evening, it had been with the intention of telling Mr Knowles definitively that they had no future together. He could not have made it easier for her.

It was nevertheless a bittersweet victory. She was no less full of regret than she had been before—no less alone. She wended her way through the gallery, keeping an eye on Kitty as she went, until she reached the couch at the far end of the room. She sat down, wondering forlornly what might have happened had she stood up from this spot one minute earlier on Monday and encountered Mr Darcy face-to-face instead of passing behind him as he climbed into his carriage.

There was little point in speculating she supposed, for she would never know. Just as she would never know what might have happened had she not been separated from him at the dinner table when they dined together at Longbourn last autumn, giving them no opportunity to converse. Or what might have happened had her sister not eloped, or had she not rejected Mr Darcy's offer of marriage, or had he not separated Jane and Mr Bingley. Their association was so dotted with ifs, almosts, and maybes that the addition of a few more misses this week ought not to have made any difference—yet they did.

She wished she had called his name when she saw him

on the street. She wished she had not hidden behind a pillar when she saw his sister. She wished she, and not Kitty, had been here at the gallery when he came yesterday. She wished she had not spurned his offer to love her.

Someone sat down next to her, and with a mumbled apology for having inconsiderately sat in the middle of the couch, she slid sideways to make room.

"Do not move away on my account, Miss Bennet."

Elizabeth's head snapped up faster than Kitty's had earlier, her heart in her throat, for she knew *that* voice, too. Intimately. "Mr Darcy!"

She was half inclined to think she was hallucinating, that he was a vivid manifestation of her yearning—only then he smiled, and she knew he was real, for no flight of fancy had ever affected her so deeply.

"Good evening," he said.

She smiled regardless of her discomposure, for it was exactly like him to make her feel so much with so few words. "Good evening," she replied.

She scarcely knew where to look. To hold his gaze seemed too revealing, yet every time she looked away, she found herself immediately glancing back again to marvel that he was there, to admire his countenance, to confirm that she had not imagined his smile. She had not; he seemed almost unable to repress it as he said, "I cannot express how pleased I am to see you."

Alas, his countenance clouded as soon as he said it, and he added stiffly, "Are you here alone?"

"No, I am here with Kitty—and your cousin's batman,

as it happens." Elizabeth pointed to them, but Mr Darcy did not look.

"Yes, but I meant..." He stopped talking and winced slightly.

"Is something the matter?"

This appeared to surprise him. "It is heartening that you should have to ask. Are you not exceptionally angry with me?"

"What for?"

"For giving you the cut direct, here, on Monday."

Elizabeth recoiled in dismay. "That was you?"

"It seems it may have been—but...you did not recognise me?"

"I did not *see* you. What do you mean, it *may* have been you?"

"It was not intentional, I—" He frowned. "You truly did not see me?"

"No. I was standing over there, lost in my own thoughts, and the next thing I knew, a lady I had never met before informed me I had been given the cut direct and began attempting to remedy all my worldly problems."

"Lady Tuppence Swanbrook?"

"Yes! Do you know her?"

Mr Darcy's smile had returned, in wry form—a slight upturn at the corner of his mouth that was wonderfully familiar. "I have just left a dinner party at which she was a guest. I never spoke to her before today, and our first meeting did not go well, for she recognised me instantly as the man who gave her new friend the cut."

He turned serious again. "After all the ways I have insulted you in the past, I would not blame you for believing me capable of it, but upon my word, it was not intentional. I saw you and was unsure whether you would wish to speak to me. I ultimately decided it was unlikely and left, but my indecision meant I hesitated. Until half an hour ago, I had no idea I had made it look like a deliberate slight. Fitzwilliam told me you would be here. I came directly to beg your forgiveness."

A powerful feeling of affection blossomed in Elizabeth's breast. She already knew Mr Darcy was capable of a great many good things—generosity, forgiveness, and gallantry not least among them—but she was nevertheless astonished by the humility of his coming to her in this way, leaving a dinner party halfway through in his impatience to speak to her and then publicly acknowledging his faults.

"There is nothing to forgive," she told him warmly. "You only looked at me. Lady Tuppence may have mistaken it for a cut direct, but I assure you, the world in general had too much sense to join the scorn."

"You are certain of that? Her ladyship seemed to think you had been censured and derided as a result of my actions."

"Yes, she was quite determined that it spelled disaster, but I have returned to this gallery nearly every day this week, and I promise, I am as uninteresting to these people as most of the paintings."

Mr Darcy chuckled lightly, and Elizabeth felt a thrill to hear it. "I understand she was given the cut direct herself once and suffered cruelly for it," she continued. "I suspect it has coloured her view of things. But I know you would never willingly subject me to that—not when you have done so much to *protect* my reputation, and that of all my family, with your unexampled kindness to my sister. Ever since I have known what you did for Lydia, I have been most anxious to acknowledge to you how gratefully I feel it."

He frowned doubtfully. "I was under the impression that you despised me for condemning your sister to an unhappy marriage."

"Despised you? For saving my sister from ruin? How could you ever think I would despise you for that?"

"Mrs Wickham told me you did."

Elizabeth's shoulders slumped, and a tiny huff of incredulity escaped her lips. With her reckless, selfish behaviour, Lydia had inadvertently done more than any other person alive to destroy her chances of happiness with Mr Darcy. To learn that with this lie she had directly and deliberately impeded their understanding was maddening.

"It cannot be a surprise to *you* to hear that Lydia does not always tell the truth," she said sadly. "Is this why you thought I would not wish to speak to you—because Lydia said I hated you?"

"You must not lay all the blame at your sister's door. We both know I have given you plenty of reasons to think ill of me."

"None for which I had not forgiven you long ago."

An expression of profound pleasure suffused his face. "I

shall not deny how welcome those words are, nor how seriously I have doubted them. I confess, I thought I must be the intended target when I heard you had expressed relief at your sister's new husband having no friends in high places to persuade him against her family."

Elizabeth grimaced contritely. "I did say that. I am ever so witty, have you not heard?"

He laughed more fully this time, but then fell silent. Elizabeth took advantage of the hiatus to cast a quick look about the room to ensure Kitty was still safe. The exhibition had begun to empty as the evening drew to a close, with only one or two couples still milling about, and she very quickly established that her sister was not in this chamber.

"I can vouchsafe for Mulhall's probity," Mr Darcy said. "Your sister will come to no harm."

Elizabeth knew she ought to search for her regardless but desperately wished to stay. She could almost have believed that with this reassurance, Mr Darcy was attempting to ensure she did, except once she had thanked him for it, he did not say anything more. Fearing that, having made his apology, he would now go, she tried desperately to think of something to say that would keep him there, but just as she decided she would enquire about his sister, he surprised her by asking about hers.

"Is Mrs Malcolm well?"

And with that one question, Elizabeth's hopes soared, for she did not think for one moment he was interested in how Jane fared. He was making polite conversation—and

Mr Darcy abhorred polite conversation. Which must mean that he wished, as keenly as she, to stay exactly where he was and talk to her.

"Yes!" she rushed to say. "Yes, she is exceedingly well. Thank you. She is expecting her first baby."

"That is happy news. Are she and her husband situated close to Longbourn?"

"No, they have a house in Buckinghamshire. Mama is bereft, but Mr Malcolm appears to be bearing the separation remarkably well."

He looked only vaguely diverted. "Is he a good brother?"

"He is a vast improvement on my first attempt."

That earned only a faint smile. "And Mr and Mrs Gardiner? Are they well?"

"They are. They have—"

"Do not marry him, Elizabeth."

"What?"

His pretence dissipated; he went from smiling and nodding distractedly at all her answers to looking at her with piercing intensity. "Knowles. I beg you would not accept him. I could give you a hundred reasons why not if I thought you wanted to hear them, only please, do not marry him."

Elizabeth stared at him, her heart racing at such a pace it was nigh-on painful. She hardly dared believe what she thought he was saying, but oh how dearly she wished to! "I do want to hear them," she whispered.

"Hear what?"

"Your hundred reasons."

He searched her face as though trying to ascertain her thoughts, then seemed to give up the endeavour with a small shake of his head and the sweetest smile Elizabeth had ever seen.

"You will hear them all and more, but there is really only one that matters. I do not want you to marry him because that would mean you could not marry me."

Elizabeth gasped quietly, then bit her lips together in an attempt to contain the swell of emotion that rose up in her. "In that case," she said as collectedly as she could, "you might like to know that I was not planning to marry Mr Knowles."

"You were not?"

"Not at any point."

His relief was unmistakable, as was the strength of his regard when he reverently took up her hand and held it in both of his. "Does this mean you will agree to marry me?"

Elizabeth could not repress the happy laughter that escaped her lips, nor the ecstatic smile that stretched her mouth from ear to ear, nor the vigorous nodding of her head. "Yes! Yes, I will!"

She had never seen any person look as happy as Darcy did then. She was used to him being more economical with his expressions, and she marvelled at how well heartfelt delight suited him. So apparent and profuse were his feelings, it was not much of a surprise when they spilt over, and he stood up, pulling her to her feet with him. She knew not whether he meant to spin her around the room in a reel or pull her into an embrace. Neither did he, apparently, for he ended up somewhere betwixt the two, standing toe to toe with her, his mouth inches from hers, and his eyes on her lips.

The last thing Elizabeth wished was to put any space between them, but she had only narrowly evaded one scandal and had no wish to stumble directly into another. She stiffened, unsure what to do.

"It is well," Darcy said in a low voice, and he gestured to the rest of the room with a glance.

She turned her head and exhaled in relief to see that her concerns were unwarranted. But for the warm glow of countless candles, the soft music floating in on the air from another room, and the watchful faces of a hundred portraits—and them—the upper east exhibition room was entirely empty. And Kitty was right again; it was quite the most romantic setting Elizabeth could ever have imagined for being reunited with the man who completely owned her heart.

She turned back to Darcy. He was waiting for her, his happiness undiminished, his smile unwavering, and his heart laid open. She brought her hands to rest upon the lapels of his jacket and tilted her head up to his.

He cradled her face with his hands. "Only a cad would kiss an unmarried woman in a public gallery."

She gave a small hum of agreement. "But you are my cad. And I love you."

The fervour this induced in Darcy did indeed add an undertone of roguishness to his kiss, but Elizabeth did not object in the slightest. By the time Kitty and Sergeant Mulhall found them, both expressing their surprise to see Mr Darcy there, they were returned to their previous, respectable attitude on the couch.

Elizabeth's new knowledge of her future husband's rakish capabilities—and her enjoyment of them—was an exceedingly happy discovery but not one she would like to be widely known. Better it was kept a secret how well Elizabeth Bennet liked a cad.

CHAPTER TWENTY

I t had been agreed, before Darcy left for the gallery, that Fitzwilliam and Georgiana would be conveyed back to Darcy House in Rutherford's carriage. He was not surprised, therefore, when his butler informed him upon returning home that both were waiting for him in the drawing room. He knew they would be anxious for him and was sorry to have kept them waiting this long, but he hoped his news would be more than adequate compensation.

He felt a palpable surge of exhilaration at the prospect of telling them. Saying it aloud, being congratulated for it, must, after all, make it real. After such a long time despairing of a joyous outcome, Darcy had suffered more than one moment of doubt on the journey home. He had taken to rolling the hair pin in his pocket between his thumb and forefinger to assure himself that he had not fallen and hit his head on the way to the gallery and dreamt the whole scenario—that he truly was engaged to Elizabeth.

A better piece of evidence he could not have wished for, obtained as it was in the transcendent moment that he finally took Elizabeth in his arms. Their union had been a long time coming, and though brief by necessity, their kiss had been unguardedly and magnificently passionate as a result. When Darcy guiltily plucked the loosened pin from Elizabeth's hair and held it up for her to take, she had told him to keep it. He had not cavilled. He was considering having it framed.

He made his way to the drawing room and entered to discover Fitzwilliam and Georgiana sitting in silence. His entrance startled them both, but once they had seen him, neither seemed willing to speak first. They watched him without saying a word as he walked to the sideboard. He turned his back on them to pour a drink, smiling to himself as he did. Were he of a disposition in which happiness overflowed in mirth, he might have made a greater show of his announcement, but his happiness was a more contained, intense business. He felt abuzz with it, as though if someone were to poke him, they might receive a shock from all the elation coiled inside him. His glass filled, he sauntered over to lean against the mantel. His sister and cousin glanced at each other nervously; he pretended not to notice.

Fitzwilliam cleared his throat. "Did you, um…did you manage to speak to her?"

"I did."

"And?"

He took a sip of his drink and savoured the feel of its gentle burn as he swallowed. His first toast to the certain bliss he had just secured for himself. "She is engaged."

Fitzwilliam swore quietly.

"But did you tell her about Mr Knowles?" Georgiana asked. "Does she know he is not to be trusted?"

Darcy nodded. "I told her."

"And still she means to marry him?"

"Oh, no." He smiled broadly—because he could not refrain from doing so a moment longer. "She means to marry me."

Darcy's disposition might have prevented him from wild celebration, but Fitzwilliam's most certainly did not. His congratulations, likely fuelled by the quantity of wine he had drunk that evening, were instantaneous and intemperate.

"Thank the Sovereign's holy orbs for that!" He leapt from his chair and slapped Darcy on the shoulder, hard. Then, apparently of the opinion that this was not celebration enough, grabbed both his upper arms and gave him a quick, sharp shake, crowing in his face. Then he let go and marched to the sideboard to pour himself and Georgiana a drink, rambling further, vaguely inappropriate felicitations as he went.

More sedately, Georgiana rose from her seat and came to Darcy, holding her hands out for his. "You brute!" she said laughingly. "We have been in agony waiting for news! You have been so wretched this year, I knew not how we might comfort you if things did not go your way." Her fond gaze and happy tone belied her stern words, and she surprised him completely by leaning forwards to kiss him on the cheek. "I could not be happier for you, Brother. Nor could I have wished for a better or a kinder sister."

Fitzwilliam arrived with two more glasses and gave one to Georgiana. "A toast! To Darcy and Elizabeth! Together at last!"

Darcy raised his glass with them, though he was too affected to say a great deal. He had never wanted anything as fiercely as he had wanted to make Elizabeth his wife, but he had not realised how dearly his relations wished it for him, also. Their heartfelt rejoicing was deeply touching and made Elizabeth's affection every moment more valuable.

"I hope your evening was not completely ruined by my sudden departure," he said to his sister.

"Not at all," she assured him. "Lord Rutherford was excessively concerned for you."

"Nevertheless, it was ill done. I shall send him a note tomorrow. I would not want him to be put off by your brother's ill manners."

Georgiana ducked her head coyly. "Thank you—although I am sure nobody thought you were ill-mannered."

"Lady Tuppence did," Fitzwilliam remarked. "But do not concern yourself—I believe she thought it made you more interesting."

Darcy would not ordinarily have concerned himself in

the slightest with the opinion of someone so wholly unconnected to him, but he thought he could see something in
his cousin's expression that suggested Lady Tuppence
might not remain unconnected to him for very long. "Since
I should not like her to tire of my company, I shall
endeavour to continue being ill-tempered for as long as she
knows me."

"I do not think Elizabeth will allow that," Georgiana
replied with a knowing smile.

Fitzwilliam toasted again to that, and Darcy was
subjected to a bout of teasing on the subject of Elizabeth's
power over him, to which he had no objection whatsoever.
He also did not regret that they parted company shortly
afterwards; he was prodigiously grateful to them both for
their encouragement, but there was too much to be
thought and felt about all that had happened to be in
company much longer.

"I am truly delighted for you, old boy," Fitzwilliam said
as he donned his coat to leave. "I look forward to meeting
her again. When are we calling on her?"

"*I* shall be calling on her in the morning but—"

"Excellent! I shall be back here at eleven."

"I shall not be taking anyone with me."

"Of course you will. You need me."

"I assure you I do not."

"And I assure you that you do. How else will you get
her on her own? I shall come and suggest a walk, then
discourage everyone but her sister from coming. And while
I am filling Miss Catherine's head with praise for Mulhall,

you and Elizabeth can find yourselves a bit of shrubbery to get lost behind."

Darcy was on the cusp of condemning Fitzwilliam's crude insinuation, when a memory of Elizabeth's sweet embrace earlier that evening persuaded him against it. He nodded. "You may come."

"Thought so!" Fitzwilliam said with a wink.

He winked again the next day, over his shoulder, from where he walked ahead with Elizabeth's sister.

"It is delightful to see your cousin again," Elizabeth said. She had her arm looped through Darcy's, and every now and again, she rested her head on his shoulder to emphasise whatever sentiment she was expressing.

Darcy was in seventh heaven.

"Georgiana is impatient to see you, also, but I am a very selfish creature, and I was not prepared to share you today."

Elizabeth looked up at him, her bottom lip caught guiltily between her teeth. "I am all anticipation of making myself the best sister she could hope for, but it is just as well she did not come today, for I am sure this path is not wide enough to admit three."

The path could have fitted two barouches abreast of each other. Darcy smiled and squeezed his arm to his side, pressing her hand against his ribs with it. "I have missed you more than I can put into words."

"You do not need to put it into words. I understand completely, for I have endured the same misery."

"I am sorry I did not come back. I wanted to. If you

only knew how many times I have almost ridden to Long-bourn just to see your face!"

"Why did you not?"

Darcy directed Elizabeth off the main path towards a more isolated one. "Lady Catherine lied to me. When she relayed her conversation with you, she painted a very different story to the one you told Lady Tuppence, and which I heard last night. I knew my aunt was angry, but I still thought her visit to you must present the very worst of her behaviour. I did not believe her capable of such malicious deceit, and so I did not question her report."

"Lady Tuppence has been of infinite use, despite her best efforts to invent an argument between us. But how on earth did you learn of my meeting with her cousin in the first place?"

Darcy was then obliged to explain his unpardonable eavesdropping. He could easily perceive that Elizabeth was amused by his absurd lunge behind the pillar but loved her all the more upon seeing her check her laugh. It was his turn to be amused when she admitted to having made precisely the same leap for cover upon seeing Georgiana in the same seat the next day.

"I ought never to have tried to interfere," Darcy said. "I like to think I *had* learnt my lesson in that regard, but when I thought you were in danger, I could not stand by and do nothing."

"We will not quarrel for the greater share of blame annexed to this week's mayhem. Your meddling may have set the ball rolling, but *my* schemes embroiled everybody from your sister to Colonel Fitzwilliam's batman in the fray."

"Perhaps, though I do not think there will be many complaints. Georgiana and Rutherford have got off to a famous beginning, and if I am not greatly mistaken, Fitzwilliam is already half in love with Lady Tuppence."

"'Tis a truly fortunate ending, in that case, for my sister has quite determinedly set her cap at Sergeant Mulhall as well." She smiled at him affectionately. "None of them will be as blissfully happy as we will, of course, but they will make do, I am sure."

"Nobody could ever be as happy as I am, Elizabeth. Not even you."

"Do not be too sure. I have not told my mother yet."

Darcy chuckled, revelling in being able to enjoy Elizabeth's wit once more. He slowed their pace, for they had reached the most sheltered part of the path. "Your aunt and uncle seemed happy with our news."

"Oh, they are—so very happy! They were convinced, when you helped Lydia, that you had done it for me. They were almost as disappointed as I was when you did not come back for me."

"They were right, I thought only of you." He stopped walking and tugged her gently to face him. With his thumb, he traced her cheekbone and jaw. "I have thought only of you for a very long time, dearest, loveliest Elizbeth."

When he bent to kiss her, she wrapped her arms around his neck, and he responded heatedly, pulling her tightly against himself. She was warm and supple in his embrace, and she fitted herself against him as though they had been made for each other. He was loath to let her go.

"Do not make me wait long to marry you, Elizabeth. What say I apply for a special licence? We could marry tomorrow."

Elizabeth rolled her eyes and encouraged him with a nudge to start walking again. "Do you know many bishops?"

"My uncle does."

"Do not be absurd. I have no more desire to delay than you, but a common licence will do."

"But if we had a special licence, we could marry in the British Institution." He was not serious, but her vehement response nevertheless took him aback.

"Absolutely not!" she cried. "I am sick to the back teeth of that place. A church ceremony will do perfectly well."

Darcy gave a small grunt. "Very well." After a moment, he added, "I bought the couch, though."

She looked askance at him, then laughed lightly. "What?"

"The exhibition is closed now—last night was the final showing. I sent an enquiry this morning and received a quote by return. It is all settled. The couch on which we were reunited will be delivered to Darcy House tomorrow. I thought it might make a poignant engagement present."

"And so it will!" she agreed, resting her head on his shoulder in another show of sweet affection. "We shall be able to finish what we started on it."

Darcy turned to regard her in astonishment, and it was

evidently enough to make her realise what she had implied, for a deep blush overspread her cheeks and she stammered, "Not *that!* I meant our marriage!"

Conscious of not embarrassing her further, Darcy turned his gaze back to the path, trying prodigiously hard not to smirk. When they had gone a few yards along the path, he could not resist adding, "After all that, it turns out *you* are a cad, as well." He smiled to hear her mortified groan. "It is well, though." He lifted her hand and placed a kiss on the backs of her fingers. "You are my cad, and I love you, too."

The End

ACKNOWLEDGMENTS

Huge thanks to Amy D'Orazio for pushing me to flex my writing muscles and try something new with this story. Thank you to my wonderful editing team, Kristi Rawley and Jo Abbott. As always, I thank my long-suffering family for putting up with my anarchic writing schedule. Thanks to my Mum, for being my staunchest cheerleader. Thanks to every reader who gives this fun little vagary a chance. And thank you most of all to Jane Austen, for not yet having come back from the grave to lambast me for having so much fun with her gorgeous characters, world, and words.

ABOUT THE AUTHOR

Jessie lives in Hertfordshire with one tame cat, two feral children, and a pet husband. She loves the English language and the art of storytelling and is rarely happier than when she's wrangling with both to try and create something that might make people laugh or feel or think. She studied Philosophy and Literature at university, but it was Jane Austen's genius with words that inspired her to begin writing, and she's had a whale of a time exploring Regency England in her own historical romance stories. She believes life is too short to be serious; sarcasm is her first language, and she is a great proponent of all things silly. She is also ridiculously clumsy and cannot be trusted near anything made of glass.

ALSO BY JESSIE LEWIS

A Match Made at Matlock (*with Jan Ashton, Amy D'Orazio, and Julie Cooper*)

Epiphany

Fallen

Mistaken

Speechless

Unfounded

MULTI-AUTHOR ANTHOLOGIES

Rational Creatures: Stirrings of Feminism in the Hearts of Jane Austen's Fine Ladies